KING PENGUIN

LOVING ROGER

Tim Parks was born in Manchester, England, in 1954. The son of an Anglican clergyman, he studied English literature at Cambridge University. He spent two years in Boston, earning an M.A. in English and American literature from Harvard and working for National Public Radio. His first novel, *Tongues of Flame* (available from Penguin), won the Somerset Maugham and Betty Task awards and was enthusiastically received in the United States. Since 1980 he has lived in Italy, where he teaches English at the University of Verona and works as a translator (most recently, of two novels by Alberto Moravia, *Erotic Tales* and *The Voyeur*).

Loving Roger

TIM PARKS

A KING PENGUIN
PUBLISHED BY PENGUIN BOOKS

PENGUIN BOOKS
Published by the Penguin Group
Viking Penguin Inc., 40 West 23rd Street,
New York, New York 10010, U.S.A.
Penguin Books Ltd, 27 Wrights Lane,
London W8 5TZ, England
Penguin Books Australia Ltd, Ringwood,
Victoria, Australia
Penguin Books Canada Ltd, 2801 John Street,
Markham, Ontario, Canada L3R 1B4
Penguin Books (N.Z.) Ltd, 182–190 Wairau Road,
Auckland 10, New Zealand

Penguin Books Ltd, Registered Offices:
Harmondsworth, Middlesex, England

First published in Great Britain by William Heinemann Ltd. 1986
First published in the United States of America by Grove Press, Inc., 1987
Published in Penguin Books 1989

1 3 5 7 9 10 8 6 4 2

The events of this novel are purely fictional. No reference to any actual
person, living or dead, is intended or should at any point be inferred.

T. P.

LIBRARY OF CONGRESS CATALOGING IN PUBLICATION DATA
Parks, Tim.
Loving Roger/ Tim Parks.
p.   cm.—(King Penguin)
ISBN 0 14 01.1459 9
I. Title
[PR6066.A6957L6   1989]
823'.914—dc19   88–21890

Printed in the United States of America by
R. R. Donnelley & Sons Company, Harrisonburg, Virginia
Set in Bembo

For Rita

Loving Roger

Roger lay on my new blue rug in the corner by the television and the lamp that seemed like it always had the funny orange bubbles rising in it that he hated. But I went to work just as usual. I made myself the regular cheese and ham sandwich and took the baby up to Mrs Duckworth for the day and she didn't notice anything odd about me, I don't think. The only thing I did different was to snap on the security lock in case Mrs D got it into her head Bobby needed a change of clothes or in case she picked too many flowers in the garden and decided to give the extras to me. Because Mrs D has a copy of the Yale key to my front door.

I washed my hands carefully, made my sandwich and went out, snapping on the security lock which is an Ingersoll with two great barrels that spring into two deep holes. Roger used to laugh at me for being scared. He used to say I had a mind full of terrors and that was why I dug my nails into other people and clung onto them. I took the baby upstairs, gave Mrs D her £20 for the week and went to catch the bus.

I went to work because I thought it would calm me down, compose me, and then in the evening, after the last letter was typed and sent and my desk was clear, after the typewriter was covered and all the little objects you have to use every day, paperclips and sellotape and the like, were all arranged perfectly square along the top edge the way Mr Buckley insisted when he did his rounds, like he always would, then, I thought, I would go and tell somebody (I didn't know who, the Samaritans maybe, or Mum's vicar who said he would never throw the first stone – but it would be the police in the end) – tell them how it had been between us, Roger and me, and why he was on the rug in the corner by the TV under that nice lamp he always sneered at and called working-class taste because of the wonky orange bubbles that floated up and down and were corny, he said. He said, 'You wet your pants for the obvious, don't you? And it's the same with relationships. You eat your little heart out to have one of those obvious relationships you see on TV or read about in your saga books.' Because while I was pregnant I'd read *The Thorn Birds* and *The Far Pavilions*.

And I said, 'Oh Roger, I love you, you know I do.'

Anyway, I couldn't not go to work on a Friday, not even in these circumstances. Because Friday was the busiest. There was a notice in our room, the girls' room, and it said, 'You can be ill any day but Friday,' and when Mr Buckley showed new recruits round the building he used to point out the notice and smile and say, 'Ill on Friday, crucified on Monday.' Friday was the end. And with Roger not being there it would be worse than ever.

I was curious to see what the office would be like without Roger, and I needed a day to compose myself before I went to talk to people. Otherwise I would be confused before I started and they would confuse me even more with their questions and I would be all jitters and tears like I am sometimes and I wouldn't have made sense out of it at all. Roger said it was bloody stupid this thing I had about making sense out of things; he said all I wanted was to find explanations that would fit into my small mind. But if you can't make sense out of it when there's someone you love and hate together so much that you did what I did, then what can you make sense out of in the end? Nothing.

I said 'Nothing' to myself out loud at the bus-stop and

2

the little Indian inspector who's always there with his pencil behind his ear said, 'Doesn't get any better, does it?' I smiled at him. I never have any trouble smiling. Even when I'm in a panic.

'Snarled,' he said brightly. 'Far as Uxbridge.'

There were about twenty of us jammed under this shelter watching water trickle from the edges.

'And all the way in to Marble Arch.'

The inspector tapped the little transistor he had in his breast pocket with a grim smile, but nobody wanted to talk. They all had papers they were trying to keep from getting sodden while they read about eight more pence on a gallon of petrol. I thought, if I'd ever learnt to drive like Roger was always telling me I should, I'd have been able to take his car and drive it in and put it in the space reserved for executives. I could have saved myself the bus fare.

He has a Passat, Roger. A Volkswagen Passat, diesel. Because he says he doesn't want to have a Ford like everyone else. It was a big thing for him that, not being like everyone else. Steering clear of the crowd, he said. Making sense of things, on the other hand, was not important.

Unless I hadn't understood somehow.

We crawled along on the bus through drizzle down the Uxbridge Road and then when the conductor came I found I hadn't brought any money with me. I was in such a state rummaging through my handbag with the young black next to me watching amused and the conductor whistling and opening and closing a big handful of tenpenny pieces – I was in such a state, I thought for a moment I was going to scream. I scrabbled in my bag. There was a pile of dirty tissues, my cross with the broken chain, tampons, make-up, used bus tickets and a gas bill, but no purse.

The conductor said, if I gave him my name and address, London Transport would send me the bill in the post.

'But I'm just about to move house,' I said.

Then the post would forward the bill, he said. He stood

over me, opening and closing his hand very quickly, so that the tenpenny pieces snapped together with a sharp click like the sound of my Ingersoll security lock. He was a big Irishman with red veins in his face and he was impatient because the bus was filling and emptying all the time and him with all those fares to take.

'Write down your address, love,' he said moving on. 'Think of it as free credit. Could be a century before you pay. No interest.'

I thought of that bill popping through the letter box a century later and the smell of Roger coming out, like the smell when I worked in the hospital and the porters wheeled the trolleys down to the morgue. So then I got up and pushed past everybody off the bus and out into the drizzle and I walked the last half-mile to the office, because rain has never bothered me, and even if I caught a cold it wouldn't matter particularly at this point I didn't think.

I walked slowly because I couldn't find it in me to hurry and when I got to the car showroom, I don't know why, I stopped and looked at the Jaguar XJ they had there that Roger always used to stop and look at and once when he was in one of his good moods he had dragged me in and made me sit in the passenger seat with Bobby on my lap, while he played with the gears and made brum-brum sounds through his lips. On the showroom window it said, Best of British, Best Bargains, but the glass was wet with drizzle and the XJ was no more than a silver smear turning slowly from one side to the other on the big revolving podium they have. I wondered a moment if he and I would still have been friends at the point when he would finally have saved up enough money to buy the thing, or whatever new model there was on the market then, and whether he would have taken me for rides in it and even let me drive it, if I had learnt to drive like he kept persuading me to; or whether I would always have been restricted to the Mini he said he would help me buy if and when I got

4

my licence: so that I would be more independent, he said, and could get out more and be happy, instead of moping so much at home like a wet rag and relying on him for transport. 'The trouble with you is you *want* to rely on me,' he said, and he said it was shameful for one person to actually want to rely on another. It was like hanging a lead weight round their necks.

*   *   *

I was late. More than half an hour.

Jackie said, 'Good evening, your highness.'

Wendy said, 'Late Monday to Thursday, venal; late Friday, mortal. Confess yourself, sinner.'

She has been to university, Wendy, and after another few months or so they will move her up to Design or Marketing and they'll find somebody new for typing. She is very thin and academic-looking with no more breasts than I had before I had the baby and when she speaks to Mr Buckley or Salvatore she holds her head high, keeps her lips stretched thin and tight and talks to them like equals, and you can see Mr Buckley likes that. You can see he thinks she's going to be the bee's knees in his department when he's got rid of Jonathan; if he manages it, that is, before Salvatore snaps her up in Marketing. She's never flustered like me and she's never jolly-jolly and flirty like Jackie, but she doesn't type half as well as us either. She makes five or six mistakes every page and her fingertips are always covered in white-out. She says her mind is too active to be a good copy-typist.

'You look like a drowned rat,' Jackie said brightly, puffing alight a cigarette.

My hair was soaking. I sat down behind my desk and took the cover off my typewriter.

'You didn't get out of bed the wrong side again?'

'And bang into the wall?'

They typed while they spoke with cigarettes in their mouths, so there was no need to reply. The smoke curled up and hung stale under fluorescent tubes. I found the first letter, which was from Mr Buckley, smoothed it out and read it. Then, when I laid my fingers on the keyboard, I saw there was something wrong. My nails were full of dry blood. I closed my eyes.

Nobody had said anything about Roger yet.

After about five minutes Salvatore came flying in, hands full of papers, all bounce and energy, which was supposed to make us feel more like working. He dropped the papers on my desk and rubbed his hands together so that you could see his cufflinks flashing gold. 'My little lost soul!' he cried. 'Here at last! My favourite dattilographer.'

He's the company clown, Salvatore, and everybody hates him and loves him at the same time, excepting Mr Buckley who only hates him. Ever since the first day I set foot in this office he's always called me 'my little lost soul'.

'Roger doesn't seem to be here today, so I've to take all the typesetting calls as well. Busy, busy, busy now!'

'You won't catch me squeezing a tear for you,' Jackie said.

Then Salvatore said jokingly to Wendy, did she, by any particular chance, happen to know where the great Mr Cruikshank might be, because everybody knew Wendy had a bit of a crush on Roger and she said very primly, no, she had no idea. Salvatore started to laugh, still rubbing his brown hands together, and I thought, Roger's in my bedsit, stretched out on my new blue rug by the television; and I thought how, if it had happened in his own room instead, or pad as he used to call it when he came back from America, then I wouldn't have had to go and tell anybody about it.

Because nobody knew anything about me and Roger. Nobody was going to ask me if I knew where Roger was. Nobody knew anything at all.

The phone rang then in Salvatore's office, which was next door, and he threw up his arms saying God save us from Fridays, only you could see he liked it really.

Then after five, maybe ten minutes, Jackie said very kindly, 'What's wrong with you, love? You look moonstruck this morning.'

So I told them I was pregnant again.

Wendy didn't say anything.

'Are you sure?'

I said yes.

'And who's the father this time?'

'Same bloke.'

Jackie was really outraged then. She asked me if he still wouldn't marry me and I said no, he wouldn't, he wouldn't even live with me, but it wasn't his fault. He just wasn't that sort of bloke in the end. He wasn't cut out for being someone's husband. I tried to be really offhand about it and opened my top drawer for the chewing gum I keep there, but there wasn't any left.

'Bugger him and what kind of man he is!' Jackie said, leaning her heavy breasts at me over her typewriter. She has huge breasts, Jackie, too big even to envy. 'I'd bloodywell kill him if I were you!'

And I said, 'I have.'

*　　*　　*

To make sense of things, if you can, you start at the beginning, and that must have been the day Salvatore poked his head round our door and said would one of us girls go and show the new typesetting exec all round all the offices, and the other two made me go because they were too busy and they knew I was shy and probably thought it was a laugh to make me go. There was no Wendy in the office then, but another, older woman called Beatrice who had a posh voice and once, apparently, she used to read things out on the BBC, the radio, only she'd left to get married and now, ten years after, she was so bored she'd decided to go back to work for a bit. Her hours were different from everybody else's, ten in the morning to four, so I suppose her husband must have been a friend of Mr G's, and anyway she always said she only came to work because she got so bored at home in Surbiton.

How she got from Surbiton to Shepherd's Bush I don't know, but it must have taken yonks.

So I went down to reception to meet Roger. He was tall, Roger, and you could see that morning he was feeling very conscious of himself to be standing there so tall and blond and straight in a place he was new to and didn't know at all and where everybody else instead all knew each other and exactly what they were doing. I even remember feeling relieved to see that this Mr Cruikshank was shy and not one of those cheeky cheery types who can never understand when you've had enough.

'Miss Eastwood,' I said, and I took him from reception upstairs to Sales and Marketing where Salvatore had his office door open to watch Sally and Yvonne. They were all three talking on the telephone, which was all they ever did, all day every day, and Salvatore was spelling out his name the long way like he always did – 'S for sunny boy, A for apple blossom, L for lover or lecher,' and so on. He was wearing a silver-blue suit and waved at Roger through the open door. A thumbs-up sign. I told Roger Yvonne and Sally's surnames and they lifted their eyes and nodded and he seemed embarrassed. Yvonne was wearing her black fishnet tights as per absolutely always, with one foot up on the windowsill where Salvatore couldn't see. 'PP can guarantee the fastest possible delivery times in the city,' she was saying, and she winked at us.

In Design, Mr Buckley wanted to make Mr Cruikshank his own man before Salvatore did, and he sat him the other side of his desk and started talking about efficiency and constant checking and this being the heart of the company where its bread and butter was made and everything else was all frills. Roger nodded and nodded and I stood by the window watching traffic grind along under the bridge on the Uxbridge Road. There was a woman crouched, wiping a baby boy's mouth at the entrance to the tube station and I thought how very nice it would be, despite all what the feminists say, to have a nice baby and be a housewife, because I was bored sick with the office and fluorescent lights and cigarette smoke. Bored right to my nerve ends. I turned round and Jonathan, who works with Mr Buckley, was peeling the back off an address sticker and smiling at me.

'Did you see *Saturday Night at the Mill?*'

I said why?

'You know that Natalie Bronsky, the American dancer?'

'Well?' I didn't.

'Well, you've got a bum just like hers.'

Jonathan is about 25, from Oxford University, awfully correct-looking and neat with a little moustache that seems almost pasted there, and he has this act of keeping a dead straight face while he says embarrassing personal things to you and that moustache never moves at all.

I took Roger down to Accounts and then Typesetting, which was to be his department. He just seemed a bit blank and nervous with everybody and I thought, he won't last more than two or three months here, I bet. I felt quite sorry for him. So that when we finished up in the telex room I bought him a coffee from the machine. Five pence a cup and expensive for what it was.

'What do you think?' I asked him, swinging on the telex stool. I was wondering if what Jonathan had told me was supposed to be a compliment or what. But then he said that kind of thing to everyone.

'It looks okay.'

'You don't sound very enthusiastic.'

9

He shrugged his shoulders and I laughed. If someone's shy then I get more bouncy and extrovert. I've noticed that. My dad says I'm terrified as a mouse, but it's not true really. Only with people like Salvatore or Mr Buckley. And not even then deep down.

'You don't sound like you really want the job at all.'

'I don't really,' he smiled. 'I never wanted to work in an office.'

He won't last even one month if he tells people what he thinks, I thought. Because everybody passes on everything in this office, and then Yvonne passes it on to Mr G.

'It's not your first job, is it?'

'No.' He paused and looked up at me. 'Well, actually, yes, it is. Though I said otherwise on the application.'

The telex began to chatter. Something from Mr G's daughter in America.

'Makes a terrible noise,' I shouted.

'Yes, awful,' he smiled, and his accent was a tiny bit Midlands, but toned right down, which I rather liked.

It was the second or third week he took me home in his car. He had an old Mini then and seeing as he lived in Ealing it wasn't out of his way at all to drop me off in Acton. He stopped where I was waiting for the bus and said why not get in? Then, after he'd taken me a few times, I chose an evening my parents weren't at home and asked him in for a cup of tea. It was a terraced house we lived in on Horn Lane and the living room had green wallpaper with silver stripes and was choc-a-bloc with all the things Mum had bought to cheer herself up after Brian died and then couldn't find any room for.

No, the job was okay, he said, as jobs went; just a step down, that was all. From what? I asked. From what he'd wanted to do. Which was? He hesitated. He was sitting in Dad's armchair with his head resting on one of my underskirts waiting to be ironed.

'A writer,' he said. 'Plays. Films.'

He began to talk then, very long and earnestly, bent right forward from the chair with his cup and saucer balanced in one hand so that the tea slopped out onto his biscuits, and while he talked, getting more and more excited, his eyes took on a bright glow and seemed to stare right into me. It was one of the big things about Roger, the way he could be terribly, terribly earnest.

The point was, he should have been something more than a typesetting services salesman, he said, with his education and the ideas and ambitions he had. But it wasn't just that. It was that we were all much much more valuable than our jobs allowed us to be and it was a crying shame that someone like him had to spend his life picking up and putting down the telephone – or me banging away on the typewriter.

He'd written an article about it, he said. 'For the *Guardian.*'

'I'm okay,' I said. 'I have a good laugh really. It's just I get a bit browned off, off and on.'

But he said, no, the problem was the whole structure wasn't good enough for us: the way everything was run,, the profit motive and discrete division of labour. He talked seriously to me in a way I don't think anyone had ever talked to me before, words that I didn't even know or understand that sounded like they were from the *Financial Times*, and while he talked I watched his mouth, his wide lips that were quick and earnest, and the blue intelligent eyes. I thought he must be tremendously intelligent. His hands, now he had put the cup down, made a lot of gestures, like a politician on TV, and they were nervous and fast with the nails bitten right down. It was a question of being crushed, he said, crushed by pressures and exigencies that came from every side, only he was determined not to be.

'But you don't want to listen to me on my hobby horse,'

he said then, and he stood up suddenly to go. I said I liked listening to intelligent people; but he had his dinner to get back to apparently. He had a room in a house off Ealing Broadway and his landlady cooked his evening meal for seven-thirty every weekday.

At the door he said, 'Oh, better not mention at the office about me taking you home. You know what it's like. Everything gets passed on and they always suspect the worst.' He laughed and I said, yes, I knew, he was right, and I remember I felt quite happy he had asked me not to talk about it, as if there was something secret between us, and I watched him walk down to the front gate across the garden our dad had concreted over after the slugs ate all his peas. It was a brisk, nervous walk he had, and the moment he was in the car he shot off like a maniac.

'He'll kill himself,' I said and again I felt I quite liked him.

*   *   *

My life, before Roger, if I think of it now, seems like a kind of dreamless sleep, one of those periods you can remember so little of it's hard to believe you were really alive. In a way, I suppose, I was perfectly happy, and again, in another, I wasn't much more than a zombie, trapped inside all my little habits – like a ball, I thought of myself sometimes, a ball in a bagatelle, constantly bounced between the sound of my alarm in the morning and the cup of cocoa Mum made for me in the evening when the feature film was over and Dad was arguing with *Newsnight*. Back and forth, morning and evening, week in week out.

I was living at home then and my home was dead. It had died along with my brother, Brian, when he was killed in a car crash three years before, coming home with the boys. Brian was 25 when he died, eight years older than me, and Dad lived for nobody else but him because he was brainy and getting on in computers and a terrific scrum-half for the Park Royal Runners and he always had a girlfriend on his arm when he got home in the evening smelling of beer and cigarettes. 'Gloomy Gladys', he called me, and if ever I complained there was nothing to do in Acton, Mum always said, 'But Anna love' – because my name is Anna – 'look at Brian! Brian always finds something to do.' But Brian had his ancient Triumph Herald he was always doing up and drove off into town.

After Brian died, my dad changed his mind about retiring early. He stayed on at work and gave up the allotment and concreted over the garden as soon as the first thing went wrong, the business with the peas that happened every year and had never bothered him specially before. Then Mum went out to work too, which she hadn't done for centuries, since before we were born most probably – filing insurance policies – and nobody talked to anybody in our house any more, or at least not in the lively way we used to before.

I asked Mum if we could repair the Triumph and I could learn on it and use it, seeing as it wasn't too badly damaged – Dad had had it towed to the allotment car park right after the accident and nobody had touched it since – but she said if my father ever saw that vehicle again most probably he'd start tearing it to pieces with his fingernails, or take an axe to it; and anyway it was a disrespectful thing even to ask. So then when I gave up at the hospital and they gave me the job at PP, I just got up early in the morning for work and came home around six or seven, if I didn't go out for a drink with Jackie, and in the evening we all watched the telly in thundering silence, so that I don't think I ever missed a single episode of anything and I always knew who was Top of the Pops and who was top and bottom of the first and second divisions – and even the third when QPR went down for a season – and who would win an election if there was one, and the Grand National and the Eurovision Song Contest, which I couldn't bear and always watched all the same.

I had a boyfriend, Malcolm, who had been going out with me ever since the third year at school and had asked me to marry him about a million times, though without ever trying to take me to bed, or even kiss me seriously. Climbing and fishing were what he was into, and before Dad concreted over the garden he used to come over Sunday mornings to ask if he could dig up a few worms, because he lived in a flat in the blocks off Acton Vale where there was no grass at all. Once or twice, after Brian died, he and Dad went off together to sit under their umbrellas by the Grand Union Canal. Last year he asked me to go and scale Ben Nevis with him, but I always feel I'm going to be sick when I go up high somewhere, or like I'm going to do something mad like throw myself off, this terrific urge I have to drop everything and jump. So I didn't go.

No, the only person who ever tried to really kiss me or feel me up was Jonathan at the office Christmas party, and he did that with all the girls as soon as he'd had a single drink.

That evening Roger brought me home, I went up and looked at my face in the mirror of Mum's dresser. I just looked at it for a while and then got up and went down again. There were two things, maybe, not quite right about my face: first the lips, which are too thin and pale, and then the eyebrows, which are bushy and rather low; and I could have solved both problems easily with the right lipstick and some careful plucking, because I'm quite pretty basically I think – my nose is certainly nice – except that I always have this terrible listless feeling when I come home from work and I don't feel like doing anything.

'The point is I'm wasting my life at the office,' I said when Dad asked me what was the matter.

'You and ten million bloody others,' he said.

'Count your blessings you've got a job at all,' Mum

said. We ate take-away curry on our knees with *George and Mildred*. Mum was always talking about counting blessings and if Dad ever got angry he said, 'Count our curses, most like, count our buggering curses,' and he always refused to come with me and Mum when we went to church on Sunday.

'Buggering God,' he said, sorting through the paper while Mother pulled on her Sunday gloves one finger at a time. She had got more religious since Brian died and even went to séances sometimes, though the vicar had told her not to. She had left Brian's room exactly as it was the day he died and nobody was to change anything in there on pain of her going into hysterics and shifting everything back how it was anyway. Meanwhile, I was cooped up in a tiny space at the back of the house that just looked straight into the back of the house opposite, while Brian's room was more than ten by ten and looked down over Horn Lane, so that at least you could watch all the people in the bus queues.

But I never even asked if I could move into Brian's room.

Roger started to bring me home almost every evening and he soon got to know which were the nights Mum and Dad stayed out and then he came in and had a cup of tea and a biscuit and I was always careful to rotate the biscuit packet from one visit to the next so nobody would know.

I don't know why, but I didn't want to let my parents in on Roger just yet, Dad seeing if he was left-wing enough and Mum weighing him up in the marriage scales and saying he wasn't a patch on Brian. Partly I was afraid they would frighten him off and partly I wanted to have someone completely to myself for once, not like Malcolm who was pretty much part of the family now and came just to sit and watch television even when I wasn't there.

So that in a way, I suppose, I was as much to blame as he was; at least at the beginning.

'Mr G's a real demon,' Roger said, dunking his biscuit, 'the way he plays everybody off against each other. He's a strategist, a real bastard.'

But I didn't want to talk about the office. I thought maybe seeing as he took me home so often now, Roger must be beginning to like me, and perhaps soon he would kiss me when we stood up and went to the door. But he didn't, just sat there in the armchair, leaning forward, talking and talking.

'No, he's the classic example of someone who's redirected all his creative powers into simply bothering other people. That's what the system does – not only makes slaves out of one half, but prison warders out of the other. The thing about lunchtime drinking, for example. He wants to control us every minute of the day.'

I wondered if he had noticed how I'd started wearing make-up these days and plucking my eyebrows to a thread and buying myself three hundred different kinds of those pantihose they advertise on the tube that cost a fortune, but he didn't mention it.

'Are you putting him in a play?' I asked.

'Mr G? I'm thinking about it.'

I asked him then what his play was about, but he said you had to be very careful about writing plays, because if you got the subject wrong, then you could waste an awful long time messing around writing the wrong things – or you could even get the subject right, but go about it in the wrong way. And that was just as bad, he said. So at the moment he was sticking to articles which sometimes they published and sometimes they didn't and otherwise he was concentrating on making contacts.

He always stood up to go just ten minutes or so before my parents were due back. Because there was the dinner his landlady was cooking. He slipped on his raincoat over the office suit: the thing was to be a rebel within the system, he said. You had to keep your job because you needed

money and keeping your job meant all sorts of acts of
slavery but deep down inside you should never accept
them. You should remain absolutely yourself.

I thought at the door he might kiss me, passing so close
while I held it open. But he didn't.

'You'll kill yourself, the way you drive,' I said.

He grinned. He had big white sharp teeth when he
grinned and dimples in cheeks that were still boyish.

'Maybe we could go out to dinner one night,' I said and
he said yes and hurried off.

Before he climbed into the car he always made this silly
army-style salute back to me where I stood on the doorstep,
as if he was tipping a hat he didn't have.

*   *   *

'You should get yourself a boyfriend, if you're so bored
then,' Jackie said.

'I never said I was bored. And anyway, I do have a
boyfriend.'

'No you don't. Not you.'

'Yes I do. I have two.'

'Oh, she has two now! Tell me about them then.'

'One's a writer,' I said, and she said, 'Go on!'

It was the pub at lunchtime and the scene was this: us,
the secs, all over in one corner, and them, the execs, all in
the other, and it didn't matter how matey they were in the
office we always sat separate in the pub either side of a
great haze of smoke and clatter of voices and dishes, because
this is one of those big Irish pubs they have in West London
where they ladle out tons of wet shepherd's pie day in day
out and those offensive-looking sausages that burst out of
their skins – 'circumcisions', Jackie calls them. While I was
talking, I could see Roger sitting in their group with
Yvonne and her fishnet black tights.

'He *is*, I'm telling you.'

'What's he like?'

'Okay.'

'Have you been to bed yet?'

'None of your business.'

'So he's not a real boyfriend yet then?'

'He's real enough to me.'

'I wouldn't be surprised if Yvonne and Mr G didn't get it on on the carpet after hours. It's thick enough.'

'I don't go for men with beards,' I said, and Jackie laughed and when she laughed she always giggled and her breasts heaved and she said it wasn't their beards I ought to worry about, oh no! And I went red as a beetroot, like an idiot, like I always do.

It was waiting for Roger to kiss me that I must have fallen in love with him. I never thought about making love in particular, nor what there might be in his trousers, nor if he would marry me nor anything like that: I was just waiting for a kiss, for some sign that he liked me, that somebody apart from Malcolm was paying me some attention, somebody intelligent and sensitive like Roger, and not a pig like Jonathan or Mr G who would have had your pants off even before they'd noticed the colour of your eyes. While I was waiting for him to kiss me and he was talking and talking, I watched him hard as I could for any sign he was noticing me, and so it was I grew familiar with the strong quick lines of his face, the close-set intense blue eyes, the straight, just slightly wide nose and the mouth that moved and moved and moved with a thick strong lower lip and a thin pale upper one and two front teeth that weren't quite perfectly straight. I dreamed those teeth.

And I grew familiar too with his gestures. While he spoke he would push his right hand into his hair and hold it there tight, gripping a handful of hair, so that when he took it out again it would stay standing up in a big shock of blond and he looked like a schoolboy. Then the other thing he did, if he was sitting at a table, was to prop up his chin on the palm of one hand with the elbow resting on the table and put his fingers in his mouth and lightly scratch those uneven teeth.

I liked these gestures. I liked the way he seemed so totally wrapped up in what he was saying that he didn't notice what he was doing with his hands. He didn't seem self-conscious at all. And he didn't seem particularly conscious of the room we were in either and never made any comment on all the rows of glass ornaments my mother had covered every horizontal surface with, so that dusting had become a sort of life sentence with picking them all up and wiping them one by one and trying to find enough room to put them all back again. Sometimes I think my mother needs to see a psychiatrist with all her whims and the way she says she's going upstairs to have a chat with Brian and goes and sits in his room for hours and hours and cries and laughs – only of course it's me most probably they'll be sending to a psychiatrist now, and I'm as right as rain, I know I am. I'm not even going to pretend I'm crazy or anything.

Before it happened he said, 'You're sick, you are. You're sick the way you draw everything into yourself, the way you never never never let be. You're sick because you can't adjust your trash literature expectations to the world as it is. To me as I am. And you eat your little heart out with that sickness and suck blood out of everybody else.'

And I said, 'But I love you, Roger. You know I do. How can you say . . .'

'You love an idea of me,' he said. 'You don't love me as I really am. You don't love the me that's struggling, fighting and adventurous. You don't have a brave love. You want me as a failure, bled dry and white as a statue, posing traditionally by your side forever.'

'We're not in a play, Roger,' I said. 'You don't have to be so eloquent.' But he started to shout then and said, there I was again, there I was, always trying to pull him down to my level, and he started to laugh and shout together, almost in a frenzy, and he said, 'Going down, madam, third floor, second, first, ground, here we are, ground floor. Oh sorry, sorry, madam, it was the basement you wanted, was it? Here we are then, the basement, plastic flowers, romantic novels, all guaranteed over 600 pages, the very furthest pavilions, videos of the royal wedding, inflatable husbands to take to church with you.'

The baby was crying all through those last moments we had together and neither of us moved to comfort him, but that wild, unrestrained cry of his seemed to fill the room so full that we were pushed and pushed into a corner with no escape whatever.

I began to cry too.

'I do love you as you are, Roger. I love every inch of you. It's just that I'm tired of not knowing how things will be tomorrow, how I will manage.'

'You will never know exactly how things will be with me,' he said. 'Never, never, never. Because I'm not a statue. I'm alive. Got it? Alive. And that means I can't be pinned to any walls. Do you understand? I can't be made sense of.'

I was quiet a moment then and we both sat there all dressed up for work with the clock ticking on and on and the baby wailing and wailing and it was time to go almost.

'So leave, then,' I said. 'Leave. I don't want to see you again. I don't ever want to touch you or have anything to do with you again. Get your stuff and go.'

'No,' he said. 'That's stupid.' And then he said, 'You'd only come crying back to me after a couple of days anyway, like always.'

And it was true.

He was sitting at the table where we'd eaten breakfast with one hand clutched in his hair and the other twirling the bread knife round in his fingers. It seemed wherever he sat Roger always started to twirl the nearest thing to hand round and round in his fingers. Behind him was the new blue rug I'd bought to cover the floorboards in the corner and the TV with the lamp on top that had the bubbles rising and rising in its orange liquid.

I was weeping and furious and quite quite at the end, and I stood up and stumbled round the table and grabbed the knife from his hands so that it was pointing at him, at his chest.

'I'll kill you then,' I said, not meaning it at all.

And he said, 'Oh, I shouldn't do it with the knife, lovey.'

He looked into my eyes and his own were laughing. Our arguments didn't even seem to touch him any more. 'You're not strong enough for the knife. I'd use the shotgun, if I were you.' Because he had a shotgun, Roger did. He had shown it to me and it seemed he had made some kind of pact with himself that he would commit suicide the moment he was quite certain that he had failed in life. By putting the barrel in his mouth. That was how stupid he could be about his ambitions and things.

He looked into my eyes and looked away to gather the crumbs from his breakfast plate, as if I wasn't worth even a moment's more attention.

So I killed him.

I didn't know I was killing him. I just pushed the knife forward into his white work shirt as hard as I could and then let go of it at once, even before the blood came. I walked round him and picked up Bobby from his cot and walked out of the back door into the garden, rocking him from side to side to make him quiet. I must have closed my eyes and ears and heart to Roger, because all I saw was Bobby's pudgy face, too young to resemble anybody else's, and all I heard were the baby's cries and whimpers and blubbering as he quietened down and I didn't see or hear anything of Roger at all.

Still, if I think of it now, it seems pushing that knife was the only thing I ever really and truly did in my life; the only thing that was truly an action in the way Roger used to talk about dramatic actions and how important they were and different from the things you did every day.

Perhaps because it was the only action I never ever dreamed I'd ever do.

*   *   *

Mr G had started the company from scratch and owned it one hundred per cent and all his energy went into it night and day. He was a gangly man with a thick red beard he could never stop touching and stroking, and despite his family and his wife, who was a nice friendly Scottish woman, not at all bad-looking, it was a sort of company tradition that he would be having an affair with one of the girls in the office. In the past it seems he had always had an affair with the girl who was his own personal assistant, but just after I arrived, Mr Buckley had advised Mr G not to take on any more personal assistants because it was such a problem sacking them when the affair went sour. Mr Buckley had been 'head-hunted' from some highbrow part of the civil service to add some brainpower to the company, because Mr G had a pretty low opinion of Salvatore, who had been his very first employee more than fifteen years before. Anyway, Mr Buckley said that it would be better to abolish the job of boss's PA altogether and for Mr G to go and have his affairs outside the company and when he needed any secretarial work done he could just send his letters up to us girls in the typing pool; or if he needed someone to arrange something he could ask one of the executives to do it. Mr G agreed because there had been an awful scene when the last girl, Muriel, left; she had stormed through all the rooms screaming obscenities and pulling down her dress over her left shoulder to show a bruise she said Mr G had made – he was a filthy, violent, disgusting pig, she said, and she was going to make damn sure the whole world knew about it. So then Mr Buckley had had to spend more than an hour on the phone to keep the thing out of the local newspapers and he had to promise that PP would spend more than a thousand pounds in advertising over the next six months, which was crazy because hardly any of the company's clients were local.

So Mr G agreed not to have any more PAs and there was a period when, when he wanted to do a letter, he would call one of us girls down to his office and walk up and down, stroking his beard and dictating and changing his mind and starting again and deciding not to write the letter after all and then telling you all sorts of personal things you didn't really want to hear and talking about company philosophy and how working for PP wasn't just a job but a way of life, like being part of a family, and if we didn't feel like that about it then we may as well pack up our stuff and get out now.

He liked to be generous and would tell Nadia, the girl on reception, to pop across the road for coffee and Danish pastries, so that the switchboard would be blocked for five minutes and everybody upstairs would be nodding and winking and saying, oh ho, Mr G was entertaining one of the secretaries again, and Mr Buckley would put on his weary professional's look and grimace over the order-book. But the point was, of course, that Mr G couldn't have his affairs outside the office because he spent his whole life in the company, and anyway, that was half the excitement of working for him. Everybody seemed to understand that perfectly, excepting Mr Buckley.

So for a while he invited all of us secretaries down turn and turn about, and then the girls from Sales too, because they were all expected to know how to take shorthand and type, and we took his letters down and listened to him talking and defended ourselves as best we could over coffee and Danish pastries, refusing offers to go for drinks after work at his club in Notting Hill Gate.

'Work has to be an integral part of your philosophy of life,' he told me in the middle of a letter about some catalogues for trade fairs. 'I mean, you're not married, are you, you're not even in love, I suspect,' and he smiled his very wide, quite mischievous smile. He wasn't an unpleasant man, just a bit creepy sometimes if you weren't feeling up to it. It was to do with his gangliness and smile, the big eyebrows and the way he kept rubbing his fingers in his beard, quite violently sometimes.

'No,' I said.

'And are you religious?'

I said yes and no, but not really.

Then what on earth was I living for? he demanded.

I faltered. The thing about Mr G was how he could make you feel you were failing in some important exam, and if you didn't do a bit better he'd hit you or rape you or something.

'I don't know,' I said hoarsely. 'But then I don't see why you should have to know really – what you're living for, I mean' – and although I couldn't have imagined it then, this was to be the answer I would always use with Roger when he started insisting I do something with myself, with my spare time, something positive, or when he said I should change my job, re-train, get into a career, because the way he saw it I was only too ready to spend my whole life pretending I was in a romance and trapping the first man who would fall for it into getting me pregnant and installing me over some kitchen sink washing nappies and so on. I laughed, because he wasn't harsh at all the way he said things in the early months, and I said you didn't wash nappies in the kitchen sink actually, in fact you didn't wash them at all these days, and anyway I didn't see that you had to know exactly what you were living for and why. It would be a terrible world if everybody went around knowing exactly what they were living for. Could you imagine that? 'Oh yes, I'm living for this. Oh, are you?

No, I'm living for that myself you know.' As far as I was concerned, I said, I was happy enough just being around and enjoying myself when I could.

The stupid thing was, though, that even though I'd meant this more or less when first I said it to Mr G, I didn't mean it at all when I said it later to Roger. Because I knew perfectly well what I was living for when I said it to Roger. I was living for him.

'So, you don't think it's important to know what you're living for, eh?' Mr G said, and I said no, and then after a moment he started to laugh and rub his beard and he said yes, well, maybe I was right, who knew, we were all rather elemental beings in the end, who cared, and he brought down his big hand in a soft slap on my knee.

There was a very short silence before I said, 'We were at, "Delivery within ten working days of confirmation of your order as outlined . . .".'

I mentioned Mr G and the office now because it seems that everything that happened between me and Roger happened in a way because of the office, or at least had something to do with it. We only met as lovers outside the office of course, but it was PP we were always talking about and sometimes I think if we hadn't worked in the same place and shared the same subjects to talk about, perhaps two people like me and Roger would never have got together at all because there would simply have been nothing for us to say to each other.

Roger was wrapped up tight as tight in his plays and articles and ambitions and he wasn't the kind of person who would think to ask you questions about your own life to draw you out. But from when he definitely decided that, seeing as he was obliged to spend most of his day there, he might as well write his play about our office, there was always loads for us to say to each other because he always wanted to know what had happened between so-and-so and so-and-so and what I thought was really going on between these two and those two, and it was fun for us to sit in our living room in Horn Lane and talk about how long it would be before Mr G got bored with Mr Buckley's wise advice and went back to his old self-made-man's happy-go-lucky way of doing things; and whether Salvatore mightn't go away and start a similar company of his own, seeing as he seemed to carry the whole sales department on his back and was the only one who had good relations with all the clients.

So it was that the first time we spoke to each other about sex was when Mr G stopped calling all the secretaries down to his office turn and turn about and concentrated entirely on Yvonne with her black stockings and long neck and the kind of bras and blouses that let the nipples show through.

'Terribly ordinary taste,' Roger said.

We were in a traffic jam near the lights with Askew Road.

'You couldn't even put it in a play, it's so obvious. Nobody would laugh.'

'Do people have to laugh?' I said.

He watched the cars, scratching his teeth.

'And then she was so obviously asking for it, it's painful.'

'But she is good-looking, bodywise, I mean. More than me.'

He stared out of the filthy windscreen. 'No, the thing is, a girl like Yvonne, he knows he won't have any trouble getting rid of her. She's not about to fall in love with him just because he's been to bed with her, or even get emotional, just bitchy.'

'Why not?'

'You can see, she's too much in love with herself to get attached to anybody else. Anybody who dresses like that is. When they do it, it's not even something they do together, just something they both do, if you see what I mean.'

So I said, 'Have you had many lovers, Roger?' and I

wondered if I had managed to keep the faint tremor in my throat out of my voice. But he only laughed, as if he hadn't heard, and he said that was precisely why Mr G hadn't wasted any time at all with me, because he'd seen right from the start that I was too serious, a much more dangerous cup of tea than Yvonne altogether; and I couldn't decide whether this was supposed to be a compliment or not.

I think every girl around 20 wants to fall in love probably, and probably every boy too, and with me it wasn't just because I'd been conditioned by a lot of romantic novels and TV, nor even because otherwise my life was so dull at the time. No, with me it was simply that Roger was very handsome (everybody in the office was saying how dishy he was) and there must have been some special chemistry he had that attracted me. He was handsome and intelligent and he had interesting ambitions and I thought with a man like that I could feel proud and in some way I would have slipped out of the mainstream that took you to where my parents were, bricked up with their glass ornaments and the television like buried pharaohs ready for their journey into the next world. But then the other thing maybe was this great capacity to love I feel, this tremendous sense of warmth that smothers me sometimes, that makes me want to cry; and I did feel this warmth toward Roger with his nervous gestures, his sense of being trapped in a job he didn't want to do, his desire to make it, not to let life slip through his fingers, the intensity he had when he talked to me from glowing eyes and said things I didn't always quite understand. I felt this love for him and I thought I was 20 already, near enough 21, and I had never been in love with anybody before and never been to bed with anybody, not even Malcolm who always talked as if it was quite decided we would be getting married one day and it was only a question of settling where we would go for our honey-

moon, down to the Cornish coast where he could fish for
bass, or up to Scotland where he could climb Ben Nevis –
I felt this love for Roger, and I wanted him terribly, just to
fold him in my arms and hug him – and even now, after
all that's happened, that still seems honest enough to me.

*   *   *

When he took me home in the car in the evening, it worked
like this. I finished work around five forty-five and went
downstairs to clock out. The typesetting office was on the
ground floor and his desk was facing the clock, so he could
see me punching my card through the glass door. If he
wasn't there I went through and spoke a moment to one of
the keyboard operators until Roger came and saw me and
realized I was on my way. Then I went out, crossed the
road and walked down to my bus-stop and after maybe
ten minutes or so he would come by in his car and pick me
up. We never actually planned this or spoke about it to
each other and the very first time he saw me at the bus-
stop and stopped for me it must have been quite by chance.
But after a while we both knew it was an arrangement.

I sat in the passenger seat watching him drive and the
truth was that he drove with the same nervous intensity he
had when he spoke and talked to you about work and
books and life and how difficult it was to do anything
serious and yet still have the money to live decently at the
same time – because he didn't want to be a Bohemian or
anything like that. He drove fast, left hand switching from
gear stick to driving wheel and back again, and whenever
there was a queue for a traffic light he would always sneak
up the line on the inside or the outside to try and steal a
march on everybody else, and when he failed he cursed
and said London was impossible and the time you wasted
getting from A to B, or even A to A +, was a crime against
civilization, because life was too precious to spend it in a

traffic jam, just as it was too short to spend the half of it hanging on the phone talking about the number of 'ems' in someone's data sheet on vulcanized rubber or whether Baskerville italics were more persuasive than Imperial bold when it came to selling vaginal deodorants.

I giggled and said, 'Oh Roger, why don't you take life as it comes? Relax!'

But he said life wasn't to be taken as it came, it was to be pushed where you wanted it to go, to the limit.

So wherever he went he was always in a terrible fury to get there and all the time between one place and another was something he regretted as if it was his own blood you'd sucked out of him. 'Only animals don't mind about time passing,' he said.

It was to be the same later when we became lovers. He wanted to do everything, to work, to buy a new car, to write, to keep in trim physically, to make love, to catch something especially good on television, everything, and he would hunt across the twenty-four hours in each day looking for spare moments he could do things, and then as soon as he was doing one thing his mind would already be hurrying on to the thing he was supposed to be doing next. I remember, there were times when we made love together that mentally it seemed he was already miles away, rewriting something he wanted to rewrite, reading something he had to read, watching BBC's *Play of the Week* and *Play of the Month* and trying to decide after the first ten minutes whether it was worth watching right through. Nothing was more infuriating for Roger than watching something right through and then thinking he could really have turned it off after the first ten minutes. It drove him mad.

If animals were the only ones not to mind about the time, I said, then maybe they were the only creatures who were truly happy. But he laughed and said happiness wasn't one of the things he was especially interested in.

I was in love with Roger and I stopped going to the church youth club and told Malcolm not to visit me any more. I think my mother was more upset than he was really, because Malcolm was very sympathetic with her and one of the only people who would put up with her stories about séances and how she knew Brian could hear her when she spoke to him, though the truth was Brian had never listened to her even when he was alive.

My father said I could have done worse than Malcolm. He had never seen anybody catch more fish in the Grand Union than Malcolm did, and if only they were edible and didn't have oil pretty well bubbling out of their eyes then he could have set up a business and made a fortune.

But when it came down to it, my father didn't care in particular one way or another about what I did. He had never been in the habit of caring about me because he had been so busy doting on Brian and after Brian died he found it impossible to switch all those affections and have me as a substitute. He tried to sometimes, but he couldn't. It was as if all the interest he had in life had been drained out of him.

Malcolm himself was very stiff about it and he said he understood (though I hadn't explained anything) and I must do as I felt, though he was sure I would come back to him, and he pecked a cheek goodbye.

I was in love with Roger. I saw him everywhere. Every blond man that passed, I turned to check if it wasn't Roger. I dreamed his soft earnest faintly Midlands voice and felt his touch the first time he would kiss me. He had to kiss me! If time was so precious to him and still he was willing to drive half a mile out of his way to bring me home and then spend twenty minutes or so over tea with me once or twice a week, surely in the end he would kiss me and we would go out and dance together somewhere.

After helping Mum with Saturday morning shopping I went back upstairs to Brian's room and sat wedged on the windowsill watching the umbrellas blow by in Horn Lane. I imagined hints I might give him to spur him on, because for all his rushing and hurrying and dynamism and earnestness, I had a feeling Roger might be quite shy with girls, perhaps had never had a girlfriend at all for trying to fit in so much else.

Millions and millions of things I imagined: kisses in the car, kisses in the cinema, Jackie's face when I told her I was marrying the dishy Mr Cruikshank and leaving the office *tout de suite* because we were buying a flat near the BBC where they had accepted Roger's play. Millions of things.

Like I said before, Brian's room was still exactly the way it had been the day he died, smothered with photographs of rugby teams that is, plus two posters of Marilyn Monroe and another of a Ferrari racing car. Even the *Playboys* and *Penthouses* under the bed had been left where they were and got dusted by my mother as respectfully as everything else, because Brian's room was by far the cleanest in the house now.

Sometimes I got out the *Playboys* myself for curiosity's sake and stared and stared and read the stories. Did Roger think of me like that? Did I think of myself like that? Was I jealous? Should I *make* Roger think of me like that? I remembered Brian, how he used to bring home his girl-friends and go upstairs and lock the door and how he must have made love to them on this very bed. But I wasn't eager to make love to anyone, I didn't think. Sometimes I thought I'd like to have children, but I wasn't eager to make love to anyone. And anyway, none of this seemed to have anything to do with being in love with Roger and waiting for his first kiss, which was less a kiss really than a sign, I suppose, a sign that he had noticed me and I needn't worry.

But Roger didn't kiss me. What he did do was to start

bringing me some books to read. Formative books, he called them. The kind of things you absolutely couldn't do without. One was a book by a man Galbraith, and another by T. S. Eliot who I had read and never understood at school. *The Four Quartets*, it was.

'Since when did you become such a big reader, then?' my mother wanted to know when she found me perched by a drizzly window pane in Brian's room.

'You never liked reading,' she said, and she said, 'Why don't you come downstairs and keep your dad company. You can't hang around here like a lost soul all weekend.'

Which meant *she* wanted to.

'Anyway, you know we can't heat upstairs as well as down. You'll catch your death.'

I read and read and got nowhere it seemed – nowhere with Galbraith, which I could follow up to a point, but then the whole thing began to make me tired, and anyway I wasn't terribly interested, and nowhere at all with T.S. Eliot, because it simply didn't make a word of sense: so what I did was to read over and over all the bits that Roger had underlined, so that I could mention them if he asked me questions. It seems stupid to me now, and especially stupid if you think that books like that are just a question maybe of practice, like doing some sport or other; but when he first gave me those things to read I was afraid that if I wasn't able to talk to him about them, he would think I was empty-headed and unintelligent and he would never take me seriously at all. So that I remember one night I deliberately avoided having him take me home in his car, because I was afraid he would start discussing all that stuff and I wouldn't know what to say. Afterwards, though, I was angry with myself and I thought the hell with him and his boring books and I waited for him as usual and said I thought Galbraith was a bit naive when it came to talking about women and what he said about controlling prices was what the last Labour government had tried to do and failed, wasn't it?

But Roger didn't even seem to be listening. He asked where had I been the previous night, because he had waited for me for fifteen minutes and he had particularly wanted to see me, because he had bought me a hat.

'A what?'

'A hat.'

He stopped the car and leaned over to move a few things round in the back – because the back of Roger's car was always a chaos of stuff thrown in at the last minute in his great hurry to move from A to B – and out he came with a huge paper bag and, inside, one of those great round felt hats. We were sat parked half on the pavement along Acton Vale in the rush hour and he leaned across and squashed the thing onto my blow-wave and twisted round the rear-view mirror, so that I could see myself, or a bit of myself, and I burst out laughing from the relief of not having to talk about those books, and quite instinctively I leaned across that space and kissed him.

So that in the end it was me kissed him first.

But not to tell anyone, he said.

'Miss City Girl, eh,' my mother said. 'It'll spoil in the rain you know,' and my father said he thought those things had gone out of fashion along with black-and-white films and I'd be better to put my money in a building society with the interest rates the way they were these days. It was one of the big things my father always said at union meetings apparently, that the working classes were deliberately encouraged to throw away their money so as to keep the consumerist fires burning, while the middle classes invested and then pounced.

But I liked my hat. It sat very cockily over my eyes, which are blue, and set off my hennaed hair – plus I hadn't paid a penny for it.

'Very chic, I'm sure,' Jackie said.

'My boyfriend,' I said.

And she said, 'Get him to buy you a skirt then, love. You're a bit short on skirts, aren't you?'

*   *   *

When we first made love, it had to do with Mr G funnily enough. And office politics.

There was a trade fair in Hammersmith where they were going to be showing a lot of computers and Mr G particularly wanted to buy an office computer, it seemed, so that he could lay off a few workers – me most probably. So he was eager to go to this fair, only he wanted to go with somebody who knew something about computers. Mr Buckley knew most about computers, but Mr G didn't really like Mr Buckley any more. He knew Mr Buckley was good at his job and terribly terribly meticulous, but he didn't like him at all, and he didn't want him to get an upper hand in the company; because Mr G is one of those people, Roger says, who, in surrounding himself with other people, always makes dead sure that he keeps all the authority to himself (in fact one of the best scenes in Roger's play was supposed to be where the Mr G figure fires the Mr Buckley figure while the PA, Mr G's mistress, weeps half-naked in the background). So the only other person who knew anything about computers was Roger, or at least he said he did to get the afternoon out; but then Roger always knew a bit about everything, because he read every page of the newspapers and remembered every line he read and every word he heard on television and the radio. Sometimes it was terrible all the things he remembered.

Mr G was going to go with Roger then. The truth was he had rather taken a fancy to Roger because he liked to see himself as he had been in young people and he sensed that Roger had drive and ambitions and occasionally he

34

asked him into his office to have his opinion on something – though Jackie said he did this with all new executives at the beginning just to snub the more senior ones; it was all part of the old divide-and-rule policy, like threatening you with the sack if you ever told anybody else what your salary was or tried to find out theirs; and then the profit-sharing business where Mr G handed out money to the executives at the end of the financial year according to their 'personal contribution'; and again it was pain of death if you let it get out about how much you'd got. 'Keep everybody on their tiptoes trying to lick his bum,' Jackie said. 'Not that they give anything out to the secs, whatever our "contribution",' and she began to giggle.

Roger said, if they were going to look at computers and word processors, then they should take a typist along with them who could say what she thought about the feel of the keyboard, and so Mr G promptly invited Yvonne, and Yvonne went off to the loo to get her make-up right. Salvatore came in from talking to a client in reception and asked where Yvonne was and when Sally told him he went downstairs to have a blazing row with Mr G because they were up to their eyeballs in sales, he said, up to their bloody eyeballs, and Mr G had to choose this moment to drag his mistress off on one of his stupid expeditions after a piece of junk nobody needed that would be just another toy for Mr G to play with in the end, like the machine they had bought for accounts to do the payroll that had never worked properly at all.

Salvatore was the sort of person who could go and say those kinds of things without ever getting fired. He was dark and slick-looking, balding slightly with a high brown shiny forehead and sharp small eyes. He dressed awfully elegantly, or he thought it was elegant, in those lightweight suits and then pink or green shirts with cufflinks. There was a way he had of flicking his forearms from the elbow which made his cufflinks flash out, and Jonathan used to imitate it behind his back to make us laugh. He said Salvatore was like one of those people who sell stolen watches in foreign railway stations. But the real thing about Salvatore was that however corny he could be with his suits and shirts and spelling his name the long way over the telephone and chatting up absolutely everybody without exception, still he did manage to charm all the clients quite stupid; and so Mr G really could never dream of firing him and quite probably was jealous in fact, or at least he was in Roger's play.

Salvatore was furious and said if they kept mucking about with his department without even asking him about it first, then he was going to start looking for another job. But Mr G, who as soon as anybody else gets angry turns perfectly pleasant and charming, so that they feel stupid – Mr G said, of course, Salvatore was right, if there was work to be done then done it must be, and what he didn't understand was why Yvonne hadn't told him she was too busy to go; he was rather annoyed with her in fact.

So that in the end they took me to the exhibition instead, and I had positively mountains of work on my desk that needed doing.

It was a nice springish day, so in the cloakroom I put on my hat and when Mr G saw me down in the foyer, he immediately said he thought I'd been looking much better these last few weeks and he hoped it meant I was settling down well in the job. I went red and blushed and said yes, though I'd been in the job a year and a half now: Roger just stood there and didn't say anything, with his hand pushed back into a shock of blond hair.

Mr G drove a Rolls Royce with red leather because it gave the company more prestige if the boss travelled in a Rolls, he said, and Roger sat beside him in the front and I sat alone in the back. I had never been in a Rolls before and sitting on the huge leather seat with that hat on and the world drifting smoothly by outside, I remember thinking this was probably what it would be like being driven to one's wedding. It was a pretty banal thing to think, I know, but fair enough in the end, and my mind started to wander to weddings and first nights and what it would be like if you were still a virgin that night when you began to unpin your hair and your white dress beside the big bed of some seaside hotel with your husband a bit red from the booze and struggling to get his bow-tie off. People say that nobody is a virgin when they get married these days, but I'm sure it would have been that way if I had stayed with Malcolm. And even then most probably he would have gone out fishing as soon as we got down to the hotel. Because the bass only come in at night.

I tried to think what it would be like going to bed with Roger, or, alternatively, Salvatore, or Jonathan, or Mr G, and I tried to undress them mentally and rouse some desire in myself, because I was beginning to think there must be something a bit not quite right with me the way I didn't explicitly desire what everybody else couldn't stop talking about. But I simply couldn't undress men mentally. Women yes, because you get to know how a different pair of breasts or a different backside will look in one dress or another, and then the world is full of naked women, everywhere – but men I couldn't undress. All I could think was that Salvatore was probably a bit oily and Mr G rather big and bony and freckled maybe on his chest, being a redhead; but with Roger I couldn't think of anything, except that he would just be Roger. And I didn't feel any desire at all. No desire to climb out of that white dress and slip into the bed in the South Coast hotel, nor any other bed if it came to that. Perhaps because I had no idea then of the luxury that one skin against another can be.

All through the afternoon we wandered through this vast, brilliantly lit hall, listening to salesmen talk about now one computer, now another, and Mr G said he was glad they had brought me because if they bought an office computer, he didn't want one that they would need some-body super-intelligent to operate, but something anybody could handle at whatever level. Roger said yes and I could have killed him.

In fact Roger talked a great deal all afternoon about different ways of integrating a computer with the present administrative system we had in the office, and Mr G nodded and agreed and objected with his long bony fingers knotted in his beard and he played the thoughtful worried boss with a lot of money at his disposal that had to be carefully invested.

I drifted after them and sat at one keyboard after the next to bang out something they dictated, and all the keyboards felt the same to me, just like my ancient golfball at the office, only without the noise and with the addition of half as many keys again that I didn't understand at all. The one really nice thing was not having to press 'return' when you reached the end of the line and not having to decide where to split the words, because the computer did that itself. Mr Buckley always says that I split up words with about the same criteria his wife slices bread, so that would be a big plus for me.

Mr G said I had nice hands, but they'd be nicer still if I didn't bite my nails, and to Roger he said that one of the advantages he'd noticed through the years of switching from manual to electric typewriters was that your secretary could have long nails and varnish them, which he always found rather attractive, and Roger laughed and said yes, who didn't? I could have throttled him and I thought how completely wrong I'd been about him that first day when I'd thought Roger would never even last a month with the company, feeling the way he did about the job. Instead it turned out that he was better at hiding his feelings than all the rest of us put together, and what's more, he seemed to enjoy it. Even if he was always in a great rush to get home after work. Perhaps it was the first time that I had a clear

sense of Roger's being a frighteningly complex person, a
sense of being put on my guard, and that just at the moment
when it was all about to start.

The exhibition was in the Cunard Hotel and when it
closed at six Mr G insisted on treating us to a drink in the
bar. He was rather merry now and at the bar he put his
arm round my shoulders and said the only trouble with me
was that I didn't enjoy myself enough. I ordered a dry
martini because it was the most expensive thing I could
think of off the cuff.

'No, I like to see some new young blood in the company,
the trouble is, if you keep the same people all the time,
things tend to get a little stale, lack of imagination, fresh
approach, you know.'

And then he said, come to think of it, he had been
meaning to ask Roger if he would like to go out to the
American office where his daughter was for a spell, because
business was looking up there and they could use someone
like him. It would be a good experience to have.

Roger's eyes shone.

The point was there was a vacancy over there at the
moment and he had been meaning to send Yvonne, only it
seemed now that Salvatore couldn't spare the girl.

'I'd be delighted to go,' Roger said in his slightly Midlands voice, and he tipped back that blond head of his to
drain a whisky and soda.

I don't know why, but the idea that Roger might shoot
off to America just at the moment he had given me the
sign of buying me that hat and I had kissed him – the idea
really upset me. The company office was in Texas, and for
me that meant sunshine and swimming-pool girls and I
thought, all on his own in a place like that he would be
bound to go and fall in love with somebody. Our own
relationship had so much to do with traffic jams between
Shepherd's Bush and Acton, drizzly evenings and quick
cups of tea, it seemed so tenuous and delicately shaded and

to depend so much on the circumstance of our both working in the same office and both travelling home in the same direction, that I felt the hot Texas sun would wash it all out immediately and he would forget me before you could blink an eye.

When we got back to Shepherd's Bush and switched to Roger's car, I burst out crying. He hadn't even managed to get the thing into gear before I was crying and crying, fiddling for handkerchieves.

He sat with the engine running and didn't say anything. It was maybe a whole minute before he said, 'What's the matter, Anna?'

'You,' I said, and I told him. I told him I spent every moment of every day thinking about him. Because I loved him. And I didn't want him to go to America. I loved him and loved him.

He sat there with his hand in his hair and his eyes hesitant and worried and then he said, 'Anna,' and reached that hand out to me. It was a purely instinctive reaction then when he touched me. I shifted myself across the seat and hugged him and started to kiss him like I'd never kissed anybody before and he was cold at first but then slowly warmed up and began to kiss me back and one of his hands went to my breast, or what I had of breast then, and he was quite violent, but I didn't mind.

We must have stayed there five minutes like that with the Mini's engine growling and grumbling like it did and my heart thumping like a tom-tom, because all of a sudden I realized I was like everybody else, I was kissing passionately in a car.

When we separated he began to drive without a word, driving more quickly and nervously than ever, only he didn't turn off when we came to Horn Lane.

'This is where I live,' he said ten minutes later. It was one of those nondescript streets in Ealing that might have been any London suburb. On Wednesday evening his landlady was always out at her cinema club, he said.

So he took me in, with me clinging to his arm, still halfway between joy and tears, and he led me straight upstairs and we fell on the bed and kissed and felt and undressed each other clumsily and made love passionately and painfully and messily, as if something was exploding inside us both – and then at half-past ten I had to go because his landlady would be back any minute.

His landlady had specifically said about not taking girls up to his room.

*   *   *

My heart beat like a tom-tom for weeks and weeks and every Wednesday evening when he drove me home, he didn't turn off at Horn Lane but kept on for Ealing. We had a hamburger in a place called Dinkies and then when his landlady would be off to her cinema club, we went to her house and climbed the stairs together to his bedroom.

I want to say something about Roger's bedroom, something I didn't realize at first, but which seems obvious now; and this was how little, or again, in a funny way, I suppose you could say how much of him there was in it. It's difficult to explain. He'd had this room for two years it seemed, since he came down from the Midlands where his family lived – his father was a plumber and sidesman at the Methodist church, his mum worked on the cosmetics counter at Woolworths – and yet he hadn't hung a single picture on the walls. I asked him why and he said he didn't have time and anyway it wasn't permanent this room, it was just a step on the way somewhere, and if he settled down and put up pictures and things then it would be like a defeat, like accepting that he was going to be in this suburban Ealing house for ever. Anyway, he had a theory about pictures and ornaments, he said. You put them up when they were fresh and new and you enjoyed them, but then of course they just stayed the same for ever, day in day out, and they petrified you in a way with their being the same.

I knew what he meant up to a point I think, because of course there was my mother with our living room packed full of those odd elongated glass ornaments that it was pain of death to move; but I said the way I saw it an empty room didn't change any more than a full one, did it?

He laughed. He said an empty room was all potential, that was the point. Bare walls were full of possibility and you had to wait till you had exactly the right picture to hang on them, if you ever hung anything at all. But better hang nothing than the wrong thing.

I said nothing. I was desperately in love with Roger in a perfectly blind, first-love way and there seems no point in describing it, because you either know what I mean or you don't. I was in love with him and I thought he was terrifically intelligent and when he said things like, 'Bare walls are full of possibility,' I didn't try to understand what the words really meant but just let them echo in my head with their intelligence and their slightly Midlands accent I had come to love.

The other thing about his room was the desk. The walls were bare but the desk was full, piled high with papers and dictionaries and books he was reading and things he was trying to write and in the middle of all this confusion there was the typewriter which he had learnt to pick on very fast with two fingers. Papers seemed to overflow from that typewriter and then spread out across the desk and down onto the floor even. On the bedside table was a dictaphone he spoke into during the night if he woke with an idea or a dream that was striking. And by the dictaphone there was the alarm clock that went off at ten o'clock, giving us just half an hour to be up and dressed and gone before his landlady came back. I don't know why, but I never disputed that I should be gone before his landlady came back.

After we had made love, which was terribly, tremblingly exciting for me those first times, so that it seemed it must be the most important thing in the world, Roger lay on his back under the sheets, naked, one hand under his blond hair and his straight nose in perfect profile against the twilight through lace curtains, and I cuddled beside him and we talked.

About his future mainly. He had this project and that project and he had made this application and that one and it was only a matter of time before something really came off and he could get himself out of the crappy job at the office.

I said laughingly, I bet as soon as he became a big success he would leave me right away for one of those glamorous actresses with the pointed tits and Oxbridge accents there seemed to be so many of on the BBC. And he said laughingly, of course he would.

'You sod!' I tickled him and he laughed all the more, squirming, and said why didn't I go and get myself famous then, so I could run off with one of those Baryshnikov types, all muscle and bum and big drooping eyelashes.

But sometimes he went sombre instead and he said we had to be very careful not to come to grief with getting too attached to each other. You had to be very careful if you weren't to come to grief, he said.

When Roger laughed he had dimples in quite peachy cheeks and he looked like a little boy – but when he was sombre his forehead went thick with wrinkles and he might have been 45. He lay on his back quiet and I smoothed out the wrinkles and stroked his body – I liked to move my hand lightly across where his chest slipped down to the flat of his stomach – and I told him not to worry because I wasn't getting too attached; far from it, I was already bored in fact and I was thinking of accepting an offer I had had

43

from Mr G and another from Salvatore and it was only a matter of time before I made up my mind. So then he started to laugh again and we hugged and talked about the office.

Till the alarm went off.

He drove me home and when he set me down in Horn Lane I felt like dancing. I felt like dancing and swirling and waving my arms and doing a jig all on the pavement in Horn Lane. Then in those first weeks the business of hiding it all from everybody seemed like a great game and I really enjoyed it when Roger came into our office and we talked to each other in an ever so matter-of-fact office tone; I even called him Mr Cruikshank once or twice, though that was probably overdoing it a bit.

'You're bright today,' Salvatore said. 'Won the pools? Busy, busy, busy now, you can't waste all day grinning like an idiot.'

I suppose it must have stood out a mile really that I was in love, with all the pretty clothes and make-up I was wearing and the occasional pirouette I did in the corridor. I felt like kissing everybody. I even put my arm round Jonathan's shoulder when I took him his letters back. Jonathan had started dictating his letters on tape these days and at the end he used to leave little messages like, 'Wanna come home with me tonight, baby?' and 'Voulez-vous coucher avec moi, ce soir?' and stuff like that. He did it with everybody of course, but I had never felt easy joking with him about it before. Now I enjoyed it and I went round the office humming, 'What a difference a day makes' and 'I believe in miracles,' and all sorts of other corny things. I even started wearing blusher on my cheeks because I was so fed up with everybody calling me pale.

'You're ever so perky,' Jackie said in the Five Bells. She smoked over tomato juice. 'What's up with you?'

'I'm having an affair,' I said and I winked at her.

'The one who gave you the hat?' she asked. Then she

44

turned very serious and said she hoped I wasn't taking any risks and I said no, of course not. Actually, I think she was probably a bit jealous, otherwise she wouldn't have said something like that. She has a bit of a round face, Jackie, rather over-powdered and very jolly, but not terribly sexy. She has been married since she was 17 to an electrician who's a champion darts player and every other week she says right, she's fed up with work and she's going to have children and stay at home, but then she never does. Because she gets bored at home I think with her husband practising his darts all the time with the television on, whereas at the office she can flirt. She has a way of laughing and putting her little finger in her mouth at the same time which she probably thinks is ever so sexy. But in the end she just doesn't have the figure Yvonne has, or even Wendy in her own way.

We were having lunch with Beatrice, the one who used to work at the BBC, and she stabbed at her teeth with a cocktail stick and said you only really fell in love once in your life so I'd better make the most of it because it didn't last. She was terribly morose, Beatrice, and sometimes she would even skip a day and then say she'd just gone down town to do a spot of shopping. She said the same thing to Mr G too, never made up stories, but he never fired her; probably, like I said, because he knew her husband or some-thing, or maybe because he paid her even less than he paid us. But these were the things you couldn't know.

We sat in the pub eating our pork sausages and Beatrice piped up again and said for heaven's sake not to marry the chap, or at least not until I'd fallen out of love with him and knew where I stood, so to speak.

'I've no intention of marrying him,' I said, and I sucked the grease off my fingers and made my lips pop. 'I intend to keep falling in love till I'm 100.' Then, without waiting for any reply, I went on, 'Yvonne's really pissed off, by the way. You know she was going to go to America? Well, it seems now he's having the affair with her Mr G doesn't want her to go and he's going to send Roger instead.'

'Rubbish,' Jackie said. 'He'll never send Roger.'

'Why not?'

'Not enough experience.'

So I told her what Mr G had said when we went to the computers exhibition.

'Oh, he was just in a good mood,' Jackie said. 'He offers everybody to go to America when he's in a good mood. Even Jonathan. Even me once, can you imagine?'

I could have kissed her.

*　　*　　*

I never really got a grip on my emotions and what was happening between us, I don't think, and so I used to struggle to understand and ask Roger what he thought of this and that and what it meant really, being in love. But Roger said there was no point in explaining, nor in me trying to understand. Because there was no sense in things to be discovered: on the contrary, sense had to be invented, imagined. Everything there was was imagined, he said.

I lay naked and a bit sticky on my back in Roger's room and watched him where he had already begun to shuffle through his papers. I felt terribly sexy when I was naked and cooling after we had been to bed together and I wanted him to turn and look at me, not to talk to me while he was shuffling through those papers. Especially when you thought how little time we had together. I was already unhappy about that. At the beginning it seems you will be happy for ever and ever if somebody just kisses you, and later you think if you could just make love now and then, once a week, it would be paradise, and of course it isn't. You want more and more. And I didn't understand how he could say that such a thing was imagined when to me it was tremendously real and urgent.

So I felt sad, spread out on his sheets like butter on hot toast and him not even looking at me. For a week, three weeks, four, I'd been blissfully happy and now already I was depressed, because I saw that although he had taken me into his life, all he had done was to install me there like I was a good new thing they had put on TV which wasn't to be missed at all costs but on the other hand only happened once a week and fitted in reasonably well with his routine. He was passionate as a lion when we made love, it was fantastic, but when it was over it was over.

I said softly, 'You're really trying hard, aren't you, Roger? I mean, you really care. About your play and everything.'

He liked to work three hours a day, he said, on his stuff. It was a question of discipline. And then most of the day Saturday and Sunday.

'And what if there's just not enough time?'

There was always enough time, he said. You made time.

'But you can't do a job, write plays and have a love affair, plus all the other things you want to do, all at the same time.'

'Why not?' he said. If you were determined enough, you could do anything. You had to be determined. It was mind over matter in the end.

'Your mind over my matter?' I asked, and he turned and laughed and he was coming over to kiss me when the alarm went off.

So in the car I made him my offer, and it was the same offer I was going to go on making him week in week out till doomsday, literally: doomsday for him, doomsday for me and a pretty rotten morning for Mr G too, losing two of his staff at one blow, not to mention the publicity.

'If you really want to do those things of yours,' I said, 'why don't you stop work right away? We find a small flat or bedsit or something somewhere and you stay at home and I earn the money. Then we can be together, even when you're working, if you see what I mean. On Saturdays and Sundays and so on. Or you can write so much during the week that you won't have to work weekends and we can go out and do things.'

But right away he said no.

Why?

It didn't matter why. But then he said it was because he could never accept the responsibility of having someone else go out and work for him while he fiddle-faddled writing plays.

But they weren't fiddle-faddle, I said. Hadn't he always said they were the most important thing in the world to him?

Hadn't he?

And I was ready to believe him, I said. I really was. He was right about not spending all his life in the office if he had other talents. He should get out and risk it and I would support him. But he said I didn't understand, and he drove back to Horn Lane faster than ever, as if we were being chased.

Before I got out, I said, 'What future is there, Roger, then? For us, I mean.'

'Future?' he said.

'Yes, future.'

But he said the future unfolded every day and that was that. 'It isn't given to us today,' he said, 'to know what tomorrow will bring.'

I thought he was quoting from the Bible, but later I found it was somebody in one of his plays said that. Unless maybe they were quoting from the Bible.

When I got home my mother was sitting in the front room crying. She couldn't talk to Dad any more, she said. Every time she wanted to talk about Brian he went up the wall and refused to talk. He'd stormed off to the pub a couple of hours ago.

I sat on the side of the sofa and put my arm round her.

She is a big woman, my mother, quite the opposite of me, with big square shoulders, swollen red hands and a round, open, blowzy face. She cried into tissues. She said it made her feel her whole life was over, Brian dying like that, it made her feel that everything she had done had been done for nothing. That life had erased her, rubbed her out. There was nothing left between her and Norman now, no reason for being together once what they cared for was gone.

I offered to make a cup of cocoa. Girls are supposed to be good at comforting their mothers, but not me. I felt sorry for her, but there was nothing to say. There had never been anything terribly intimate between my mother and me. We didn't have one of those pally mum/daughter relationships where you can talk about everything. She had never even told me about having my first period or sex or anything. I had to find it all out at school and I still could have killed her for that.

I went and got the cocoa and brought it back. Mum had switched on the telly and there were two people chasing each other through back alleys and firing.

'Where've you been till this hour, anyway?'

'Out,' I said.

She looked at me from red eyes.

'You've got a boyfriend,' she said.

'It's not unheard of.'

She watched while I poured the cocoa from the pan. One of the people on the television fell from the top floor of an elevated car park.

'Why don't you bring him home? I'd be happy to meet him.'

I shrugged my shoulders.

'You're ashamed of us, aren't you? That's what it is.'

I shook my head.

'Brian always brought his girlfriends home,' she said then, and her lower lip was quivering, 'Brian was always happy to have us meet his girlfriends.'

I picked up my cocoa and went upstairs.

It was freezing in my room because the upstairs was never heated in our house, and when I got into bed I had to hug myself tight as tight to keep warm. When I had children, I thought, I would never put them before my husband, nor before myself even.

In my room there was a bookcase full of the cheap novels I used to read when I had tried to be a nurse and did nights at the hospital, plus some Snoopy posters, a mirror framed in yellow plastic and another poster which was a print from a watercolour and showed a girl floating in water in a long dress – Malcolm had given it to me because one of his sisters had bought it and then decided she didn't like it.

I watched the walls and listened to the television. It was useless living with my parents, I thought, if I couldn't help them and they couldn't help me. At least if I had a place of my own Roger would most probably stop over and make love to me every evening. Even if he didn't live with me.

Then thinking of making love again I realized I should probably have a bath with the state I was in, and so I got up and slipped on my dressing gown and went tiptoeing to the bathroom. My dressing gown is one of the nicest things I have. Black and silky with Chinese dragons. I bought it myself with the first month's money I got from PP. I looked at myself in the mirror with the dressing gown and I slipped off one shoulder and then the other and let the shiny material glide down my body and leave me naked. Roger would like that, I thought, and I did it a second time and stood on tiptoe so I could see a bit further down, because the mirror finished at sink level.

'You've had three baths already this week,' my mother shouted through the door coming up to bed, but I didn't reply. Brian used to have about a hundred baths a week with the water slopping over onto the lino, and nobody bothered him.

I went to bed and couldn't sleep with thinking of sex

again. There were some nights when I didn't sleep for hours and hours for thinking about sex and thinking especially how stupid it was to be sleeping there on my own all creamed and perfumed and dying for it and forced to hug myself on my own and freeze.

With him sitting at his desk typing away with two fingers!

He could at least have let me done his typing for him, for heaven's sake.

I was even awake at one thirty when Dad rolled in singing rugby songs. He had bought Brian a book of rugby songs just a week before he died. I remember the cover – you still see it in Woolworths sometimes – a bunch of beefy men rubbing mud off themselves in the shower after the game.

I had got to sleep and it must have been the middle of the night, I suppose, when I woke up stiff with surprise and I knew it was a sound that had wakened me. Then it came again, a faint rapping against the window. I was quite scared, but I went to the window and opened it and there was Roger of all people standing in the handkerchief of our back garden, grinning like an idiot.

'What is it?'

'Shhhsh!' he hissed and motioned for me to come down.

I slipped on the dressing gown and sneaked down our stairs which creak at every step. I'd forgotten to put my slippers on of course and I could feel bits of things under my toes crossing the lino floor in the kitchen. I unbolted the door and he came in. He was in jeans and a sweater and tired-looking and his eyes were bloodshot.

'What . . .'

'I just wanted to see you. . . .'

He was terrifically earnest and pushed his hand into his hair. With the way he did that his hair would stay on end sometimes when he took his hand away.

'Roger, but we've only just parted.'

'I wanted to tell you I care for you,' he said solemnly.

'Oh Roger.'

And I hugged him on the cold lino of our kitchen floor. Then I said, 'Watch,' and I stood back and pushed off each shoulder of the dressing gown so that the Chinese dragons slid away down my skin. He came and hugged me and kissed me and kissed my breasts and started to make a trail of kisses going down and down.

'Not here,' I said, 'if Mum and Dad hear!' Anyway, I was freezing. I bent down and grabbed the gown.

'Let's go to the car then.'

I showed him I didn't have any slippers on, but he said it didn't matter, he was parked quite near and he could carry me. So as soon as we were on the garden path he picked me up in his arms like when they carry brides over thresholds in old films. But then with holding me he couldn't manage to lift the latch on the garden gate and I began to shake with cold and laughter and he had to put me down. My heel landed right on a stone and it was excruciating, but I couldn't yell because of Dad and Mum's window only a few yards away. I limped to the car over grit on the pavement.

In the car Roger was incredibly romantic – and this was a funny thing about him. He scorned the kind of romantic books I bought sometimes and the women's magazines I read at work and he tried to limit sex and love to just a small part of his life, so as to have time for all those other things that were so important for him, and yet at the same time he wanted everything he did to have quality. He didn't want it to be just sex between us when we went to bed together, he wanted it to be passionate and he wanted it to be love, because otherwise one might as well just masturbate he said. So that he actually tried very hard I think with sex and he did his best to slow down his desire and make it something special and make sure he wasn't just exploiting me and that I had an orgasm too, even though as soon as it was finished he would be up mooching about his papers all over again and there was the clock anyway, one of those digital things with beady red numbers, paring away our moments together till I would have to go.

He was very romantic in the car. There was me crouched and shivering on the passenger seat with my feet tucked up under my bottom, knowing I was going to catch the most almighty cold because of this, and he came close and put his arms round me to hug me warm and said the point was he'd come to explain everything; that he did care for me, and he did miss me and there were evenings when he couldn't write and he would have loved to have been with me, just sitting with me or in bed with me, and many times he thought it would be wonderful if we took a flat together so that he could write more and finish his plays and make contacts and so on and so forth – only he wanted to explain why it was impossible.

I sat quiet and half-shivering still and he hugged me close and tight and buried his head under my neck a minute which was one of the things he used to like to do – 'smelling my smell,' he said – and then he started to explain.

It was to do with responsibility first. And commitment, he said. It was dangerous. What he meant was, getting into things before you were sure. And the same with writing. What if he spent two, three years writing his plays and taking them to the BBC and the theatre companies and nothing came of it? And what if we were out of love by then? If we didn't care for each other any more? And he had taken three years' money living off me for nothing.

I hadn't quite followed all of this and I said, 'But I'll always be in love with you,' and he said, 'Anna,' and he was silent.

It started to rain. The windows had all misted up and you could only vaguely see the cars parked and the houses and the cellophane yellow of the streetlights misty through our breaths on the window.

No, he hadn't explained himself at all, though, he said. There was a conflict inside him. He wanted me desperately, in a way, and some nights he couldn't sleep over it, but he just couldn't imagine us living together, how we would fit together. He couldn't see it. Perhaps the thing was he didn't know whether what there was between us was just physical or not.

I said, did it matter? and he said it did.

Very quietly then he said that he had had another affair with a girl while he was at college and he had understood at the end that it was only physical what there was between them and of course it had been appallingly difficult splitting up and he didn't want that to happen to us.

Because these things used up so much time and energy and emotion.

And then because his Methodist upbringing had given him such a tremendous sense of responsibility even if he was an atheist now. It was a hangover and there you were. He couldn't play happy-go-lucky Casanova.

I didn't say anything, but I just felt smaller and smaller and colder and colder. I honestly didn't know he had had an affair before me. The way he'd been so shy at the beginning and then the mess the first times we made love had made me think the opposite. I rubbed at the goose pimples down my calves and puckered out my bottom lip.

Then also, he hurried on – because he wanted to explain everything and everything, he said – there was money. Money was a big problem. He didn't want to live as a Bohemian, supported on his secretary girlfriend's salary and always scraping and saving. He didn't want to end up like his mother and father who considered their semi-detached in Stoke-on-Trent the top of the tree and talked about package holidays to Tenerife as if they were the apex of jet-setting and then felt guilty because they might have given more to Oxfam. No, he wanted to have a reasonable amount of money and live well and wear nice clothes and go to clubs and theatres and drive a good car, not a crappy old Mini that needed a plastic bag wrapped round the distributor in wet weather. He didn't want to feel guilty about things. He'd made a big effort to get to Cambridge and pull himself up in the world and he wanted life to have some class for heaven's sake, some style, some beauty, otherwise he might as well kill himself and have done. That's how he felt. And saying that, he had worked himself up into quite a temper. Even in the dark light there was you could see the vein sticking up out of his neck and his eyes fierce. He drummed his hand hard on the steering wheel.

'I like the car though,' I said. 'I mean, when it stops in the rain. I feel it's part of us this car. I don't want you to buy another.'

'You don't have to waste half your life trying to repair it,' he said.

It was one of the things I realized quite soon with Roger, how you simply never knew which way a conversation was going to go. He had arrived there at my house all hot with passion and ready to make love to me on the kitchen lino and now there we were agonizing over all those different things and me genuinely horrified he would sell the Mini, because only when he said that did I realize how much affection I had for the thing, and how much affection you can have for anything that is part of being in love with somebody.

'I'd like to make love,' he said, and he pushed a hand inside my gown.

'So would I, only I'm dying of frostbite. I'm going to have goose pimples bigger than my nipples soon.'

He laughed and then turned all concern. He was being pretty irresponsible keeping me freezing there in his car listening to his stupid psychological trials and tribulations: he was all set to carry me back to the house when I realized I'd closed the front door.

'For God's sake,' I said, 'I've closed the front door. How am I going to get in?'

We both sat there like a pair of idiots. 'I can't believe it,' I said and he said he couldn't believe I'd been so stupid.

'Don't blame me. You're the nut who started throwing earth on my window at three o'clock in the stupid morning.'

'How does the back door work? Is it self-locking?'

'No, there's a key and a bolt. I unlocked it when you came in.'

'And did you lock it again?'

'I don't know.'

'Well, you'll have to try it.'

'But how am I supposed to get round to the back door? There's the gate.'

'I managed it,' he said. 'How do you think I got round the back to throw the stones?'

We crossed the bit Dad had paved over at the front of the house and there was a side passage going through to the back with one of those tall narrow creosoted gates blocking the way. It was padlocked from the inside and there was even a string of barbed wire across the top – as if anyone would ever want to get in there. Bar me.

'Put your foot on the wall,' Roger said – the low wall that ran round the neighbour's he meant. 'Hands on top, between the barbs. Here, let me lift. Now right foot on the notch in the drainpipe.'

And there I was, suspended barefoot in my dressing gown from the top of the gate. Roger slithered a finger up the inside of my legs and touched me. 'For God's sake!' I hissed, nearly laughing and crying together. I'd grazed my knuckles on the wall. 'What now?'

'Find a place for your left foot between the barbs and swing yourself over.'

I did, and went crashing down the other side, getting myself a huge splinter under my arm.

'Okay?'

'There still seems to be only one piece,' I said, which was something our dad used to say when anybody asked him if he was all right.

'You've got a great bum from underneath,' Roger said from the other side of the gate.

'Thanks a lot.'

I went to see if the door was open and it was, so then I locked it from inside and crept upstairs into the bathroom and pushed open the window which looks down on the side passage. Roger was there looking up, laughing from under his blond hair.

'Goodnight Romeo,' I said, and after he had gone I realized that whatever the purpose of his visit, which I still hadn't understood really, we were much more in love than we had been before. Both of us.

'Is that you?' Mum called softly as I re-crossed the passageway.

'Who do you think?'

But I knew who she thought. She thought she heard Brian going round the house sometimes. She thought his spirit came back there. As if anyone with liberty of spirit would bother to come back to Horn Lane.

At work when we had two minutes alone, I said, 'You mean, if I was earning a fortune you'd be happy to let me support you?'

'No, of course not.'

And in another half-minute when we passed in the corridor I said, 'I'm willing to take any risk, Roger. I don't care if I lose or win.'

But he said not to talk as if I was in a bad novel.

Roger said the things he liked about me were how slim my knees were, the point of my nose, the way I shivered when he kissed my ears, and how soft I was when he came inside me. Also I pulled such funny faces.

I said I liked everything about him.

He also liked the way I walked when I was barefoot.

I said it was hilarious that we'd been making love since May and it was October now and I'd still never met his famous landlady. Didn't she ever suspect something was up?

He said the only thing she might have guessed from was the sheets, and that was why he always put the towel under us and washed it himself.

When I thought about this later at home, I cried with thinking that even the very first time together he had been prepared enough to remember that towel.

*　　*　　*

Mr G sent Salvatore to America so as to be able to keep Yvonne and have her downstairs whenever he liked without any bother. Which meant that Roger had to do extra work in Sales and Marketing as well as Typesetting and so he stayed late at the office doing some of Salvatore's work and earning a lot of overtime money. Which left me no-where. He even stayed late on Wednesday sometimes. And Friday. So I got into the habit of going to a disco off the Fulham Road with Jackie and her husband, Dereck, and some of their friends.

'So where's this famous boyfriend?' Jackie said. When she danced, her breasts swished everywhere. Dereck always went upstairs where there was a bar with a dartboard, so she danced turn and turn about with everybody and especially with a big boy called Ian who worked in a bank and was thickset with a bit of a paunch. He had one of those tiny earrings too, which was terribly funny somehow.

'He's working on a play,' I said. 'They're producing it at a local drama club.'

'Oh,' she said. 'Are you in it?'

'No,' I said.

'Can we come and see it?'

'No,' I said.

'I don't believe you.'

'Suit yourself.'

'I do,' she said, and went off with Ian again. Ian was getting divorced apparently and he needed cheering up.

I mention these discos out of all the other things I did because of the way I felt there. Which was awful and awfully excited both together. I felt awful about Roger; not just because he wasn't there, but because he wasn't there because of the office. I mean, I could understand the sacrifice when he stayed at home to write his play, because that was something important for him and so important for me too. He had read bits to me that seemed really very funny. But when he stayed at the office it just seemed like an insult. I honestly didn't want any other men but him, I hardly even thought about it, but at the same time I was angry and I wanted to dance with other men and talk to them just to show I could do it. Then I was a bit dressed up for the disco too. I had this black crêpe jumpsuit which was open at the shoulders and lots of make-up and perfume and I wore my hair blow-waved in a more glamorous kind of way with a big curl swooping down over my forehead – and all these things together made me feel very sexy in a way I never had before I started going to bed with Roger. Maybe, I think, because being in love with somebody partly means being in love with yourself, accepting yourself, feeling good about yourself, and this was new to me. I danced loads of dances, even slow ones, and I let loads of people buy me drinks and I always ordered the most expensive ones I could think of.

One night I had a boy take me home called Tony. He was a doctor, as it turned out, short but quite handsome. He was doing his internship at St Thomas's Hospital and when he stopped outside our house he switched off the engine and turned round and started to kiss me. I was taken by surprise and I let him and he started to feel me up and say how marvellous I was. The funny thing about kissing him was how absolutely the same as kissing Roger it was, except that this man's chin was a bit more stubbly.

He said, did I want to go back to his flat in Hammersmith? And with all the drink I'd had and how tiddly and dazed I was feeling, maybe the only thing that saved me was I was screaming desperate to go to the loo. Tomorrow, I said, and for some reason I shall never understand I gave him a wrong phone number.

All the next day I felt like an idiot and I stayed in all the time thinking he might drive round when he realized the phone number was wrong. My mother was furious because I wouldn't do the shopping with her and I said I was ill and she said no I wasn't, I was mooning; I was mooning over that stupid boyfriend who obviously wasn't serious, otherwise he would have had the good grace to come and see his girlfriend's parents, and as a result she would have to do her back in lugging home the whole week's shopping on her own.

'There's always the trolley.'

But she couldn't get the trolley over the kerb the other side of the Uxbridge Road, she said. Not when it was full.

When it got towards evening and I thought this Tony really *might* come and expect to take me back to his flat – I had even dressed up and everything with a smart creamy skirt, a pearly blue blouse and the only pair of cami-knickers and proper stockings I had that I'd bought for myself one of those days I was so depressed I could have climbed the post office tower with my fingernails – when it got towards eight o'clock I suddenly started getting nervous; I wasn't sure I really wanted him to come, and I put on my coat and went out. I walked down to Acton High Street, quick as I could, keeping my head down as if every passing car might be his car, and I took the 217 to Ealing Broadway and walked to Roger's.

It was a semi-detached and Roger's room was on the

side where the drive was, so you could see his window, but there were lace curtains, so you couldn't see inside.

I prowled up and down the street in the twilight and there was an Indian lying under his car who occasionally brought out his face to look at me quizzically.

I went and rang the front bell.

The landlady came to the door, an everyday kind of a woman in a thin sweater and slacks. She was about 40, I suppose, and a bit shapeless, with the kind of stiffly permed hair that wouldn't move in a gale.

I asked her whether Roger was in.

He wasn't.

Did she know when he was coming back?

She didn't.

I hesitated.

Was I his girlfriend? she asked, and I said no, I wasn't, I was just a good friend of his and I wanted to ask him to come to a party.

She invited me in to wait for him and I was so confused I accepted without thinking. She took me into the living room where she was in the middle of ironing with the radio on. And it was Roger's things she was ironing, funnily enough, moving the point of her iron round in his underwear. He had about eight pairs of the same multi-coloured underpants that his mother had bought for him in a sale before he came down to London.

I sat down on the couch and the radio was saying what a terrible shame it was somebody had died so young. Mozart I think it was.

'I think he's ever so handsome,' the landlady said and she said, 'I'm Betty, by the way, call me Betty. I always think it's rather odd he doesn't have a girlfriend, don't you? If I was a bit younger I'd have a shot myself.'

'He's not that handsome,' I said, watching the care she was taking with an office shirt.

I hated Roger then. I felt a sudden surge of anger and

hate. I hated him for putting me in this stupid position with his landlady where I had to say I wasn't his girlfriend — especially when she didn't seem the kind who'd mind him taking girls up to his room. I hated him for having people who ironed his shirts and cooked his meals for him without him giving anything of himself in return. And most of all I hated him for having gone out on a Saturday afternoon when he was supposed to be doing his 'work' without having bothered to see if I wanted to do anything.

While I sat there furious and seething, Betty decided to tell me her life story. She was a widow twice over, would you believe it? At 36! The first had been killed in a car accident and the second, a bit older, by a heart attack. Only three months after they were married, if you please! It didn't do to have a reputation of being widowed twice, she said. This man she was going out with at the moment, for example, a tax inspector of all things, he was very cagey, very. But then she was fairly iffy herself really. When you thought of all the bother it was moving house and setting up furniture and so on and so forth — just to have the poor chap go and die on you. Not to mention the funeral. Arranging another funeral would be the death of her. No, if she ever got married again it would be to somebody ever so much younger than her so as to be sure he'd outlive her. Men died so young as a rule. It was funny they called women the weaker sex, and she let out a little giggle taking a stab at the crotch of Roger's flannel grey trousers.

I suddenly wanted to go. I had to get out of there as fast as possible and dash back home in case that Tony did come to find me. Then I would go out with him and dance till midnight and go back to his flat in Hammersmith and spend the night there making love to him over and over and over again.

I stood up. 'Maybe you should have a shot at Roger then,' I said. 'It could be just the sort of arrangement he's after.'

She looked up sharply from over those trousers and I think she thought she was being made fun of, which wasn't the case at all. I meant it.

I hurried to the Broadway in time to see the back of a 217 sailing by – 'Ride the Tube,' the ad said. Then I'd waited maybe ten minutes, thinking how at every moment Tony might be knocking on our front door and my mother would be rude to him because she'd think it was the boy-friend who should have visited them ages ago, when a great metallic car crossed the road to draw up in front of me and Roger wound down the window.

'Step in, honey,' he said in a mock American accent. 'Wanna ride?'

And this was the Passat.

It seemed he had been saving up for the thing for ages, until all the overtime he'd been picking up with Salvatore away had finally done the trick. On the never-never, of course.

'But what have you done with the Mini?' We were battling through Ealing towards the North Circ.

'Dealer gave me a hundred quid for it.'

For a hundred quid I might have bought it myself, I thought.

We were halfway up Hanger Lane when suddenly he pulled the thing over onto the pavement by a phone box.

'You'd better call your parents,' he said.

Because we weren't going home that night. No, we were going to Cambridge to his old college for the night. To celebrate.

It was like Roger to make these big romantic gestures. He came out of his cave for a while and he wanted to make a big splash. He wanted to have money and security, so he had to go to the office, and he wanted to be an intelligent person and a successful writer, because writing was the only thing he really truly admired and he couldn't accept that he wasn't in some way special and admirable himself, so he had to write; but then he also wanted to feel he was really living life with a capital L, and so he had to do things like waste his money on a car he didn't need and whisk me off on romantic trips.

And that was how I got pregnant.

I hate it in books and films when people get pregnant and you can't quite understand why – why they didn't use contraceptives, I mean. It all seems so pointless. So I'll tell you exactly how it happened to me.

When we first made love that time when we dashed back to his room, we hadn't used anything in fact, just because it was so urgent and passionate and so on; and then at the end of the month there we both were biting our nails like a pair of idiots, when my period came a couple of days early, thank heaven.

So my idea was to go on the pill and have done. But Roger said no, absolutely not, because the pill was dangerous. Roger read everything about everything in the newspapers and he said the pill would raise my chances of cervical cancer in middle age by something like thirty per cent and it might make it difficult for me to have a child when I wanted one and he didn't want to take on all that responsibility. So I should use something else, but not the diaphragm or the coil, because they were both just as bad. They promoted growths. He didn't want to think he'd made me risk growths. So we went to the Acton Family Planning Centre which was on a place called Cloister Road of all things and Roger said he'd have to put that in his play. He parked there and said he would wait in the car while I went in. I walked up to the clinic which formed a dead-end to the road, and walking along I saw that every single car parked there had a man sat in it, biting his nails or picking his nose or trying to find something worth listening to on the radio. And inside there were only women.

If I didn't want any of the above then the only thing

there was was foam and condoms, they told me; but I didn't want condoms. I don't know why but condoms always give me a feeling of dirtiness. Just the thought of them, just their name and smell, but most of all the way you see them lying around everywhere so that sex just seems like part of the litter and cigarette stubs in the gutter. So that was out, I said. And they shrugged their shoulders, two la-di-da middle-aged ladies and a tiny Indian woman.

What do I do then? I asked. Because Roger had gone on and on so much about these other methods and not wanting to have the responsibility for me using them, that it seemed now that the only choice was between those horrible rubber things, or celibacy, or pregnancy. And quite everything seemed out of the question for me.

Then the little Indian woman piped up and she said, quite off the record and without promising anything or accepting any responsibility whatsoever, if you used foam on its own and made sure you used enough of it, it was probably as good as anything else. The middle-aged middle-class ladies frowned and obviously wanted to argue, but I said thank you so much and left at once, clutching three precious little cartons of the stuff.

Roger said if they said that, then okay. He hadn't read anything about foam in the newspapers. And we drove home.

On the road to Cambridge, he went slow and then fast and dipped and lowered the headlights and let go the wheel to see if the thing drove straight. Instead of following the A10 the whole way he turned off near Ware to take a tiny country road, because he wanted to see how the car handled on difficult curves and things he said. I watched his blond hair and straight nose and the vein that stood out on his neck when he pushed the thing into third round a tight bend. He was a beautiful man, Roger, very very fine, as if God had taken a great deal of care in making him, and I thought what an absolute fool I was to have been so ready to run off with Doctor Tony-baloney only a couple of hours ago. I felt guilty almost.

All the pubs were closed when we arrived in Cambridge so we went straight to the college bar where his best friend Neville would be waiting for us, he said. Neville had studied along with Roger three years before, only he had stayed on afterwards to do a PhD in eighteenth-century poetry, and when we met him in the bar which was all fluorescent lights and puddles of beer they both started to argue about which of them had done the right thing. Neville was thin and gangly and balding with popping-out brown eyes and he smoked a pipe that kept going out. He said Roger had compromised himself accepting a position in an office which was a kind of prostitution of his talents (because Neville thought Roger would have been an ace as a critic) and Roger said all Neville had done on the contrary was to refuse the challenge life offered and to shut himself away in a cloister.

I thought of Cloister Road and realized I hadn't brought my foam. And this was the first full night we were to spend together.

I nudged Roger's knee, but they were talking about the BBC now and whether they should have spent all that money on re-doing Shakespeare and Roger said the BBC was hugely responsible for the cultural malaise in England today and I think Neville agreed, but not entirely because he had written a piece for Radio Three on Dryden which they had broadcast, though nobody seemed to have actually heard it. From time to time he turned to me and asked me if I needed another drink.

It was about midnight when we went up to our room. Neville had booked Roger into one of the guest rooms, but he hadn't realized there was going to be me too, so he had only booked a room with a single bed.

'We'll survive,' I told him, and it seemed like the first thing I'd said all evening.

Still, the bed was very single.

When I told Roger he said not to worry, if we couldn't make love, we'd do something else exciting, and he put on his jacket again.

'Like what?'

'Never mind. Come on,' and we were down the stone stairs again and crossing the green with half a moon sailing through scattered clouds over spires and chimneys.

We got in the car, drove to the river, parked and started walking. Crossing a bridge we stopped and kissed and kissed and I felt myself melting. There was this fact about Roger and me, right up to the end, that when we touched each other it was like fire. I couldn't think of anything else.

'We're going skinny-dipping,' he said.

'You what?'

If he didn't cool down he was going to come in his pants, he said.

It was fairly warm, though there was a spitting of rain in the air and everything round us was shadowy and rustling. I held him and giggled and said he was crazy.

'No, come on.' He crossed the bridge, slipped through two barbed wire strands and began to walk across this sort of meadow. I followed. I still had on that smart creamy skirt and pearl blue blouse I'd put on in case Tony came to get me to spend the night making love in his flat in Hammersmith, and my high heels sunk into the ground like it was butter. I could feel the mud go over the top and wet my stockings.

Roger was a bit tiddly, I think. He'd drunk about three pints which was unusual for him and he began to undress right on the water's edge. On the other bank there was a huge lawn stretching away to a long low building with just the odd light or so and occasionally you could see a figure moving along the wall. It was really all quite eerie with the shadows and the hissing of the water sliding by. If I'd been on my own most probably I'd have been scared stiff.

67

'You'll never take your pants off,' I said.

But he did. He stood there looking very pale and white against the dark river and he came to hug me, nude against my skirt and blouse with his thing hard as hard. Then he wanted to undress me.

'I can't put my best clothes down on the mud, Roger.'

He told me to wrap them up in his jacket. He slipped the blouse off my shoulders, unsnapped my bra, kissed my breasts. He wouldn't let me do anything myself and I felt pale and vulnerable and goosepimpled to be standing there getting naked in an open field at night with a smell of rain in the air. But it was so, so exciting too.

He got down to my cami-knickers and slipped them off as well – just like Tony-baloney would have most probably, if I had given him the right phone number, if he had come round earlier in the car.

We hugged.

'Come on then.'

'You're not really going to dive in.'

'Why not?'

'But how are we going to get dry?'

'Use my clothes. Anyway, it's only two minutes to the room.'

And he turned and took a running dive.

I went to the bank and crouched there and his blond head bobbed up in the dark slow water.

'Stand up so I can see you,' he said.

I stood up straight a moment, my nipples hard with the cold and excitement, a breeze on my bare bottom, and I felt so obvious and stupid standing there if only somebody walked by on the path on the other bank, that the only thing to do was to dive in.

The water had a slippery weedy feel; the bottom was six inches of mud so that when you put your foot down you could feel it squeezing up through your toes with bits of grit. We trod water and tried to kiss. Our skins felt rubbery one next to the other. He laughed. What a way to avoid making love, he said. He had shrunk to a pea pod. I put my hands down to touch him and he touched me everywhere. Not so much out of sexiness, but because it was strange and new to be in the water together like that. An aeroplane went over and we trod water to watch it winking by. Then we swam up and down a bit and this was the best part, seeing his blond head bobbing along beside me and smiling and blowing out water, like two people happy together on a journey. Because this was the first time we had ever *done* anything together apart from work or make love.

We swam back to the bank and climbed out. I dried myself a bit on his jeans which were rough and hurt, and with being still damp my clothes wouldn't pull on properly. He kept interrupting and wanting to kiss me and he even knelt down on the mud and started kissing me in my pubic hair, but I stopped him. I was freezing. Standing on one leg to get my stockings on, the mud squeezed right up over my ankle and we rushed back to college hugging and shivering and giggling like a pair of complete lunatics.

And then I knew it was going to happen. I could see it a mile off – that as soon as we got into that warm room and that warm single bed and started hugging together there with all the blood rushing back, we were quite bound to make love the way we were feeling. Him in one of his moods of release and me simply swamped with love.

He said, 'Your period's only just ended, hasn't it?'

'Monday last,' I said.

'So you're still safe probably.'

I didn't know, I said, and we did it anyway. It was so much more exciting to do it without anything and I felt so in love with him and for the first time I had the feeling that he really did with me. We made love twice and slept close together all night. It was strange, but I felt quite re-

ligious in a way, holy even, and lying in the dark beside
him I said a prayer and meant it.

Then the next day he was black. He was in an awful, snappy
mood. At lunchtime he said he didn't want to stay in
Cambridge all day. It was a waste of time. He wanted to
get home. He had so much to do before this evening. There
was a scene he wanted to rewrite, something he had to
catch on TV.

We stayed on the A10 the whole way and in the car I
said, 'You're like Jekyll and Hyde you know.'

And he said he knew, he knew, but there you were.
What could you do? He opened and closed his hands on
the wheel which had a black leather cover and when there
was no need to change gear he sat with his left hand pushed
into his hair.

He was like Jekyll and Hyde, he loved me, and he didn't
love me. He liked being with me, but it didn't satisfy. It
didn't make him feel the person he had always wanted to
be. His ambitions had become a habit and it wasn't one
that included me. In his plans there was some other girl,
ever so intelligent, independent and undemanding. A girl
who would join in when he argued about structuralism
with Neville and who wouldn't say prayers after making
love.

Coming off the North Circ, he said grimly, 'You should
have fallen in love with somebody else.'

'Thanks a million.'

'It's too much responsibility.'

And I said, 'Fuck you, Roger Cruikshank, and your
fucking responsibilities.'

It shocked him when I swore like that. Roger never
expected surprises from other people. He thought he had
everybody taped. Especially me.

'You don't understand,' he said.

But I did. He kept the walls of his room bare and he

wanted to keep his life bare too. So as not to be trapped, so as not to have to hurt anybody tearing down one picture and putting up another. Really, he didn't want to have anything happen at all until he was sure it was the right thing. He didn't want life to be real till he decided so.

On the other hand he had ended up with me.

'Bugger off, then,' I said.

He was parked in Horn Lane.

'What?'

'Bugger off. You can't treat me like this. I don't ever want to see you again.'

'Anna!'

And I got out of the car and slammed the door.

Mum was eating chocolates over adverts on the telly.

'Bloke came round last night,' she said, and she eyed me, eating.

'Short, darkish?'

'That's right.'

'Leave any message?'

But he hadn't.

I ironed my clothes for work the next day and hennaed my hair and cleaned and polished and painted my nails. I examined a spot there was on my chin, looked at my bank statement and shaved under my armpits. But time passes slowly in our house and in the end there was nothing to do but lie there and cry till Monday. I loved him, but I wasn't going to let him wipe the floor with me. Because just at the moment he was having his cake and eating every last bit of it too. I chewed on my lips and made myself ugly crying and around nine o'clock I slipped out through the front room while Mum and Dad were cocoa-ing in the kitchen and I walked down West Churchfield Street to read the ads in the newsagents' windows. Bicycles, belly dancing lessons, bedsits. . . .

★   ★   ★

Mr G's daughter, Diane, sent a telex saying she couldn't put up with Salvatore because he kept bossing her about and trying to take over all her clients. Everybody saw the thing when they went down for their fivepenny cups of poison and Jonathan actually started a fifty pence sweepstake on what day Salvatore would be ordered home, but Mr Buckley caught on and said one more practical joke and Jonathan was out on his ear. He got onto Mr G on the phone to say it was bad practice having notes like that on the telex, visible to all. It undermined executive authority. But Mr G thought Mr Buckley was getting at his daughter and blew up and told him to go to hell with his good-and-bad-practice civil-service bullshit, so that Mr Buckley went around for a week looking like somebody had stuck a poker up him.

Then Salvatore flew back the very next Monday and Mr G sent Roger instead. He sent him so quickly that all we had time for was a ten-minute goodbye on the corner of Horn Lane and Acton Vale with the car half up on the pavement in rush-hour traffic and him insisting there was no need to cry.

'Anna,' he said and kissed me and I climbed out quick and fled before the floodgates burst.

I stopped in Woolies on the way home and bought a card called *The Parting* with a picture of two last-century people kissing by a horse and carriage. It was the only relevant thing they had. I addressed it to where he was going to be in America and wrote:

'Roger, I know you were dying to leave when we said goodbye.'

And then I wrote:

'But words can never express what you mean to me. Whatever happens, just remember I love you, Roger.

'God bless, Anna.'

I don't know why I wrote, 'God bless,' and as soon as I had posted the thing I felt what a big mistake it had been and how it would confirm his opinion of what a sop I was and how conditioned by the trash I read.

He wouldn't understand that I really had wanted God to bless him.

In Boots I bought a Predictor just as they were closing.

I'm going to put down some bits of his letters. I kept them all of course and tied them with some scraps of yellow ribbon. Exactly what I shouldn't have done, because when he came back and found them he started going on about how that was all I wanted to do with him in the end, tie him up in frills and bric-a-brac, freeze him at a single point like a trussed-up teddy bear to take to bed with me. Letters were fragments, not documents, he said, and that was why he always put the hour of writing as well as the date at the top.

April 8th, midnight

Dear Anna,

This place is incredible. I can hardly believe it. It sounds hackneyed I suppose because we've all seen it millions of times on TV, but when you actually get here the size and sheer scope of the place, the towering height of the buildings, it's wonderfully exhilarating. They're like a challenge, like monuments to ambition, as if they'd built a million Towers of Babel and just dared anyone to come and knock them down. It's all given me new hope, made me feel alive, electric, in a way I haven't since university, and the very first evening I got down and started writing. Some of my best stuff ever.

The office is on the sixteenth floor with a view right across the city glittering away as far as you can see like a great ocean of wealth and activity. It makes you want to plunge right in and get going. I even feel eager to get to work, start haranguing people, telling them PP are the best outfit in the world. It doesn't matter if it's not true (in fact it's crap), it's the gesture that counts, doing battle, you against them, the joy of conflict, like a medieval joust. For the first time I find I can look on the job as something formative that can really help me with the writing, if only I can manage to analyse how these people tick and get them down on paper. I've already sent some stuff off to an agency here. Fingers crossed. Somehow I *know* I'm going to make it though, and when I do. . . .

Diane is crazy. She dresses in crocheted little pullovers without a bra and gives all the clients the come-on. She must be screwing about a hundred of them all at once. You can see why she didn't get on with Salvatore. They're both too flamboyant and extrovert. I've been playing Mr Diligent-Ready-To-Learn-You-Tell-Me-Everything (even though she's younger than me) and she treats me like a little dog. It's pretty frustrating, but I'll sort her out sooner or later. She has the same domination complex her father has. Misdirected creativity, all energy and no philosophy behind it, so she just goes on slaying giants every day without any sense of the limited time she's got or where she's going to be when she's 60 or what life might be for. Nothing. She's trapped right inside the moment, even if she reigns there supreme. All force and no reflection.

People in general are so different here, though. I don't mean deep down, but in their surface idiosyncrasies. Take Caesar our doorman, for example, he . . .

It wasn't like he was writing to me at all. The letters were very long, but they didn't say anything particularly written for me. They were like essays. They didn't say, 'do you remember when . . .' or, 'when I come back we'll . . .'

Is it soppy to expect a man to write, 'you remember

when we . . .', so as to send you out to the bus a bit brighter of a morning?

They were typed on office paper (because Roger always stole office stationery for his own work, it was one of the few perks he said) and I wondered if maybe he didn't make carbon copies like he did with the letters he wrote to Neville, which were like critical articles, he told me, and he needed them for further reference.

I thought I had never slayed a giant in my life and I had no idea where I'd be at 60. Somewhere between Ealing and Shepherd's Bush most probably.

Life was for loving though.

I felt like I was in cold storage.

Maybe we should split up, Roger, before it's too late. I feel you're so far away. I feel so empty inside sometimes.

I was crying when I got to work and Jonathan was very kind and took me for a drink at lunch, cracking all the jokes I'd seen already on the *Benny Hill Show*. He told me I had a nice crotch and I told him he had a lot of nerve.

It's really incredibly elemental. I think that's the word. How can I explain it? You feel you're right inside a machine or some living throbbing organism. I mean, you can feel the energy vibrating all around you. There are cranes swinging everywhere. Taxis bouncing over pot-holes. Everybody's in a rush. Everybody's going some-where. It's so immediate. Maybe that's why people are so friendly. There's no time for reserve and crap like that – 'How do you do, Mrs Cledwyn-Jones, bit of a nip in the air, isn't there' – the kind of thing that makes you want to throw up in England. No, here you have to break right through and meet people before they move off again. Because everybody's always on the move, everybody. . . .

There was a divorced woman called Natalie apparently who lived in the apartment opposite his and had invited him in to dinner as soon as he arrived and told him her whole sad life story. Now she was working in a bar and studying art history at the university at the same time, which Roger admired, because art and life should interpenetrate and that was what Neville staying on at Cambridge hadn't understood, so that he was simply fossilizing really into a skeleton of critical ideas without a shred of flesh and blood on them.

Flesh and blood. I could have killed this Natalie. I could see Roger's face desperately earnest over the table while he spoke to her, so articulate, his hand pushed into blond hair, his skin so clear, his eyes so clear, so carefully made, lightly scratching his front teeth, while they sat and ate her microwave hamburgers, telling her life and art should interpenetrate and he felt marriage was a trap too.

What would you do if you were a divorced woman and Roger came to dinner all eager and fresh? Seduce him. Flesh and blood.

P.S. Why on earth did you say that about splitting up? I really miss you, Anna. I'd love to show you the city here. Why don't you come out for the summer vacation? Acton is only seven hours by plane.

I didn't understand those letters. They seemed to point in all directions at once. Or like Brian when he used to lay bets on five horses in the same race to be sure of coming in with something.

Was I his safety net? Or his long-shot jackpot?

He was already saying vacation instead of holiday, for heaven's sake!

Sometimes I felt infinitely older than Roger and infinitely more flesh and blood.

Going to bed at night was horrible.

76

'My little lost soul,' Salvatore said. 'My favourite dattilographer − and I thought you'd brightened up.'

Beatrice said she didn't want to say she had told me so.

'Ian still needs cheering up if you're interested,' Jackie
reminded me, meaning the divorced pot-belly at the disco.
Her face was perfect Cheshire cattish.

Jonathan said he'd give me a fiver if I let him pinch my
nipples.

*   *   *

So I went up to Cambridge one bank holiday weekend to
find Neville and tell him I was pregnant.

'Three months,' I said.

It was like seeing your headmaster about bad results. He
had this room which was all wood panelling, books, old
leather furniture, a threadbare Axminster and a thick stink
of pipe smoke.

Neville was lean and nervy and wore glasses now over
his popping-out eyes. He walked quickly up and down
with his hands pressed together praying style under his nose,
while I sank into the armchair with my coat on still. There
was a gas fire and the place was stuffy.

'I can't believe it,' he said for the hundredth time. 'Incredible,' and he asked me if I had ever read *The Mill on
the Floss*.

No. My mother had turned it off at episode 2.

'The point is you have to tell Roger,' I said. 'Because I
can't.'

'Oh.'

I stood up.

'Tell him I'm pregnant but I don't want to pressurize
him. He can do what he wants. That's why I want you to
write, not me.'

'But aren't you going to, er . . . I mean, on the National
Health you could . . .'

He had both forefingers pinched into his nose and then he bent down suddenly and scratched at a white ankle. Standing up he had to fix his spectacles back on his face.

'I'm not going to have an abortion.'

'Hmmm.'

As if I was a student who had said something he didn't agree with.

'The other thing is, you better give him my new address. Have you got a piece of paper?'

And I bent down and wrote on a piece of headed paper that had a coat of arms embossed at the top.

'Would you like to – er – come to lunch? We can go to hall. I'm allowed a free guest once a week.'

But I told him no.

'Tell him as far as I'm concerned I love him. But I don't want to pressure him.'

'No,' Neville said. 'Very wise.' He laughed a bit nervously. 'I suppose this is what he always meant by plunging into life.'

'Yes, I suppose it is.'

'Well, if there's anything . . .'

The place I found wasn't bad really as bedsits go in Acton and I think it was sitting there on my own in the evening without even a television that I finally grew up. Terribly quickly.

I was pregnant. The dark little chemical ring reflected quite sharply in the mirror they give you from the light coming through frosted bathroom glass. It was unbelievable. And yet people obviously did get pregnant.

I listened to LBC. This was life then. The lemon-yellow light on dusty wallpaper and all the things you have to do between one day and the next. I washed my tights in the kitchen sink. How would I tell my parents? How would I tell Mr G? What would I do if he fired me? According to a book I got in the library the thing, my child, ours, was

78

scarcely more than two inches at three months. Abortion would be a cinch, no? There was a black girl in the type-setting department who'd aborted and she said all that post-op depression stuff was crap. She'd felt fit as a flibbertigibbet the moment it was over. I remember her saying, 'fit as a flibbertigibbet,' and thinking what a funny expression it was and I should tell Roger. He liked to collect funny expressions.

But I had no trouble making up my mind. What would be the point of aborting and starting over again? I wasn't going to fall in love another time the way I had with Roger. You can't do that twice. If you could, it wouldn't be what it is. If you could, I didn't want to know. And I didn't want some lukewarm nice arrangement with a pleasant man who would be kind to me. I wanted Roger or nothing, and if I had told Neville I didn't want to pressure him, then it was only a ploy to have him feel so bad he couldn't possibly let me down. If he did let me down I'd kill him and never love any man again, ever. I loved Roger.

My feelings were so strong sometimes, it was scary. Especially when I woke at night. I felt I could tear the world apart. My skin was howling, howling, howling. I shouted into the pillow and banged my fists.

According to Jackie I was mad. The bloke was a bastard and if only I'd let her meet him she'd give him a piece of her mind he'd never forget. Of course I would love again. Everybody did. I was only 21. I couldn't know. And everybody had abortions these days. If the bloke wouldn't marry them. Or the modern equivalent of marriage, live with them. I *had* to abort. Otherwise I was done. I'd never see light again.

'But if it's destiny?'

Oh that was a good one, she said, and went off to tell Beatrice.

Beatrice said she had learnt over twenty years of marriage, not to mention the rest, that there was no such thing as destiny. Only boredom.

Beatrice worked with a cigarette in her mouth these days and let the ash drop all over her keyboard, so you could tell her days were numbered.

But it *was* destiny. I'm not religious really in the normal churchgoing sense of the word, but I'm not immoral either. I believe there is a sense to things, or if not a sense then a direction, a flow, a current, something that you can say starts here and gathers strength and goes there where it ends. Roger thought it wasn't so, he said life was absurd and arbitrary. Because death was absurd and arbitrary. Death was completely meaningless and backfired across your whole life, making it meaningless from beginning to end, and that was why he was always in such a hurry, to be someone and make something before arbitrariness caught up with him. So in his pessimistic moods he was always comparing himself with Keats or Shelley who had already written everything and were dead at his age, or thereabouts, and then in his better moods he compared himself with Golding who hadn't started even till he was 40-something. But he still had to hurry all the same.

Once I said, 'More haste less speed,' and he groaned and went and pretended to bang his head against the wall.

It had to be destiny though; and if I had an abortion I'd be lost, without sense or direction.

Mr G insisted on taking me out to the restaurant and said he wished I'd told him the day before, because he'd just gone and given Beatrice her notice to keep Buckley happy who was fuming about inefficiency.

He ordered duck for us both without even asking me and scratched in his beard.

'Buckley is a cretin.'

If I wanted any help whatsoever of any kind whatsoever, I should come to him. He had a little bit of experience in affairs of this nature and after all PP was a big family, he'd said that before.

Then he burst out laughing and spilt his wine: 'God, I hope nobody thinks it was me!'

And I laughed too. He made it a kind of celebration somehow, inviting me out, drinking wine, even though the book from the library said not to. Of all the people I told, Mr G was the only one who asked me what I was going to call it and didn't suggest an abortion.

I could take three months off when the time came and then come in part-time fifteen or twenty hours a week till I felt ready to go back to normal.

*　　*　　*

There was another letter from Roger and he obviously still hadn't got the news.

He was beginning to get fidgety in the office. The point was, yes, a writer needed experience, but even a little went a long way. Look at Proust. At a certain point there was no need to experience any more. You were ready. His memories, even of his early twenties, were enough for volumes. Anybody's were if they knew how to use them. He had been reading John Updike and admired the descriptions. They were so detailed. It made you realize you'd hardly noticed people's faces before, how every line and detail was part of their character, every fold and wrinkle. With O'Neill on the other hand it was a question of voices, every little tick was there, every slight shift in register, every hesitation (it was the hesitations sometimes that told all). Maybe in the end the thing was you had to have a sort of love affair with everybody before you could describe them or reproduce their voices, you had to be infatuated by everybody, and at the same time cold as stone, watchful as a cat.

I didn't get any nausea, which was rather lucky, I suppose, but I did feel terribly tired and heavy at the end of the day

81

with aches in my back and sides. My stomach was tightening. I lay out flat on my back on the bed and read Roger's letters. He seemed so in command in his letters, so sure of himself and intelligent.

I thought I mustn't at all costs let the baby destroy his career. Perhaps we could even use the baby as an excuse for getting his career off the ground. He stayed in the flat and wrote and watched the baby and I earned the money. I could even work part-time so that I'd be able to get back to do the cooking too.

He was gifted. He had shown me a letter from the BBC saying his script showed lots of promise. Or I could take the baby to my parents for the day, if they retired, so that Roger wouldn't have to be bothered.

I thought millions of things, lying on my back on the bed with the sound of Mrs D clomping about overhead. Millions of things. And even now, looking back, they don't really seem so stupid.

So this is how I remember my pregnancy; lying in the dark at night, sleeping badly because I couldn't lie on my stomach, listening to LBC fill up the time, planning and planning till my head ached. How many days till Roger got Neville's letter? How many days till I got Roger's? Had Natalie seduced him? Was that why he had suddenly stopped mentioning her? Did he have to go to bed with her so as to be able to describe her face and copy her voice? Was that what artists did? And what was it about art that made them so ready to screw up their own lives for it? I liked a good film or book, but they weren't that important surely? I would like it if Roger was successful, but I would love him all the same if he wasn't. Death couldn't make life absurd if you managed to make a go of it with someone you loved. And how come I had no trouble remembering his face, every little line of it, every changing texture through chin and cheek and forehead when he smiled his smile? I had pinned so many hopes there.

Mum said that when she had been expecting Brian she had felt exactly the same, exhausted, and she hadn't had morning sickness till me, only then she had had it all day, not just in the morning, which had put her off ever having babies again. She was so flustered and excited, searching in drawers trying to find where she'd stored all the baby clothes, that, standing up suddenly, she swept about ten glass ornaments onto the floor. She didn't even seem to care. She'd told me that lad was up to no good, not even wanting to come and visit. But there you were, told-you-so's didn't help anyone, did they?, even though she had, if I didn't mind her saying so. She could give me some knitting patterns if I needed them.

Dad said Malcolm would probably still be willing to marry me if only I had the humility to go and ask.

He didn't understand the modern world, he said. People just seemed to be asking for trouble.

We sat together in our front room drinking cocoa while Mum scribbled her list of all the things I'd need to buy and then crossed all of them off one by one, because she had this, that and the other herself, and if she didn't have it then she knew someone who'd just had a baby and would have it. Because there was no point in throwing money at the shops before I'd even started, was there?

Then when she found the baby things, they were all Brian's, embalmed in mothballs – they'd have gassed a poor baby in no time – and there weren't any of mine at all.

On second thoughts, though, she said, she'd keep them till it was actually born. Because you never knew what might happen between now and then.

Did you?

*   *   *

It came on a morning like any other. My hands shook. I had to drop to my haunches in the porchway.

My dearest Anna,

Of course I love you. If you knew how often I think of you, of the way you put your tongue between your teeth when you concentrate over the typewriter. Your little ears with those pearl earrings. The way you put your hand over your mouth when you laugh. I love how eager you are when you kiss. It turns me inside out. I remember watching you go up the stairs in the office once. Your legs are so slim, so delicate. Your knees are so slim.

Why on earth did you go to Neville first? Of course he immediately tried to persuade me I should break off directly and try and force you to have an abortion because we're not socially/intellectually compatible. The typical university crap. He says it's only physical what's between us and anybody can see it a mile off. But I've been thinking about it, because you remember I was worried once about it all being just physical and so on. Only I see now that you can't really separate the physical from the person. If I love you physically, I love you. If the way you turn your head, the way you slip your clothes on, your smile — if these things make me burn, then I love you. What does it mean to separate someone from their smile? It's absurd. I love you Anna. And if that means I love a person I didn't expect to love, then I must just accept that.

So let's have the baby. I'm happy. Even if there will be problems. I thought at first I should come back at once. But then I decided against for two reasons. First, I'm getting a lot more money here, which we'll probably need. Second, it's going to be pretty difficult to explain why I have to come back so suddenly. I think it would be better if people didn't know for the moment. It would put a lot of pressure on us.

I'm dashing this off before an appointment. I only just got Nev's letter.

Look, give me the number of a public phone box and a day and time and I'll call you.

All, but all my love.

Your own, Roger.

I danced to work.

'Has the brave lad offered his hand in marriage?' Jackie asked.

'No, but he loves me.'

Beatrice was clearing her desk to go, so there was a bit of an atmosphere in the office, and then just when the time came to say goodbye she burst into tears and wept and said what she'd always wanted most of all in life was a baby and she couldn't have one, never, and instead it was bloody typical that a stupid little girl like me went and had one when I didn't need it and didn't even understand what it meant, or what anything at all meant, talking the way I did. It was bloody fucking buggering typical. Because life stank. Stank, stank, stank. Shit and piss! She started shouting quite hysterically and shoved the calculator on her desk onto the floor.

Mr Buckley walked into the room and walked right out when he saw her crying and in the end Salvatore had to take her home in his car all the way to Surbiton.

The first thing he said was, 'You didn't have to send a telegram.'

I was in a phone box in Acton High Street at eleven o'clock, just the day after his letter came.

'I can't believe it's you,' I said. 'Your voice. It's so lovely to hear you. Oh Roger!!'

'Yes,' he said. 'Anna.'

'It's my first transatlantic phone call.'

'You're kidding.'

'No, honestly. I can't believe your voice is so clear.'

There was a tiny bit of a wait while we got used to it.

'So, Roger?'

'You're pregnant.'

'Certainly am. You should see me.'

'Is everything okay? I mean, you've been to the doctor's and done the tests and stuff. I wouldn't want . . .'

'Sure. I'm okay. You don't have to worry about me. The doctor says I'm perfectly normal. Everything.'

'Great. Good.'

'That was such a nice letter you sent, Roger. If only you'd said those things before. I'm so happy!'

He didn't say anything for a few seconds. Then he said, 'So am I.'

'About telling people though. Shouldn't we do it now? I mean it's a bit bad at the moment not saying who. . . .'

But he said absolutely to wait until he got back. He didn't want me to announce it. He wanted to tell people himself. When he got back.

So then I asked him how things were going over there and he talked to me for ten minutes about Diane and the office and some phone-in programme he listened to where the presenter just abused the people who called in but they loved it, and how much more free you felt living in America, partly because of the buildings and spaces, and there was some agent in New York who had written and been very encouraging, though he wouldn't raise his hopes until it was in the bag.

I was to take good care of myself and he would start reading baby books.

'I can't wait till you're back, Roger,' I said and I took his voice home to bed with me and hugged it and let it soothe me to sleep.

I had spoken to Roger on the phone and everything was okay. When he came back he would tell everybody.

The day after the phone call, when I got back from work, there was Neville sitting on my windowsill polishing his glasses. He had been to a conference in Kensington. On Pope.

He was different in my bedsit. He sat on the edge of my armchair and said yes to himself a couple of times and was very polite and respectful, but as if he was terribly embarrassed about something, and from being the headmaster you had to be scared of, he had turned into the sort you have to be ever so kind to or they might take fright and never speak to a woman again.

A bit weedy, but not a bad bloke in the end, I thought. He had dressed smart for this conference obviously, but wasn't used to the tube and had come out messy. In my bedsit with the Snoopy posters and the one of the girl floating in the weeds and all my clothes chucked all over the place in the morning rush, he looked a bit of a fish out of water. I boiled tea.

'Thanks for telling Roger,' I said. I didn't feel angry with him at all for having tried to persuade Roger to leave me. If that was what he thought was best, then fair enough. He had a right to his own opinion.

'I want to talk about Roger,' he said suddenly.

'Oh, it's all okay now. He wrote me a wonderful letter, you know, I . . .'

'I've seen it,' he said.

'You what?'

He sucked in his cheeks hard and his eyes shifted. He wriggled uneasily in his smart jacket.

'Roger and I made a pact, oh ages ago, when we were 18, a sort of agreement to send each other everything we wrote and tell each other everything that happened to us. I send him copies of all my letters and papers. I've read all the letters he sent to you.'

It was like being slapped in the face. Or finding someone odd in your bed. He had read all those letters.

'But why?'

'I suppose the idea was that it would give each of us a

source of material. I mean, in the sense that it's pretty rare for anybody to have complete access to somebody else's private life, isn't it? And we thought it could be useful from an aesthetic point of view.'

'What do you mean, material?'

He shrugged. 'To write. To reflect.'

'But he even says rotten things about you in some of his letters. He doesn't send those surely?'

'Yes,' and he laughed faintly. I was an innocent. 'Everything. You should see some of mine.'

'I've seen enough, thank you very much.'

I wanted him to go. I wanted him to get out of my room immediately. To give me time to think. I felt short of breath. It was monstrous writing a letter like that to me and then sending a copy to this polite, weedy, academic man with the popping-out eyes and queer smile.

'The point is, I just came to warn you about that letter.'

I stood up and took the cups into the kitchen.

'Anna, I . . .'

'Don't use my name,' I snapped.

'Look . . . God.' He came round the screen wall into the kitchen. 'I'm just saying, have the baby by all means, if you want, that's your business. But don't trust Roger. He's histrionic.'

'And what's that supposed to mean?'

'He acts. I mean, he has an idea about how a person should live and so he acts like that. He writes a letter which that person would write, but he isn't really that person at all. He isn't reliable. He's like Laertes when Polonius dies, all rant. When he attacks me for staying at university, for example, it's only because that's what he really wanted to do and instead he did something else and acts out a different life because of these ideas he has.'

'For a professor, you're not very good at explaining yourself,' I said. I was doing the dishes, trembling, and I wouldn't look at him.

'I'm not a professor, I'm a junior fellow.'

'He phoned me too. You can't know about that.'

'No, but that's not the point – anyway he'll tell me all about it in his next letter. No, the fact is he has this . . .'

'You're just jealous because you're losing your bosom friend to a girl.'

He came out with half a snort that was meant to be a laugh. 'I'm trying to tell you this for your sake! I wish I was losing a friend. I can assure you I'd have been a lot happier if he hadn't sent a copy of that letter to me. Can't you see how he just plays? The thing with the office. Being an executive. He plays. He's not an executive, but he . . .'

I turned round, letting my hands drip on the floor. I could feel this awful tension in my mouth and my jaws clamped tight.

'Just tell me what it is you want to tell me and then go, please. I can't bear it.'

If I think back on it now, I must say I feel quite sorry for Neville, not angry at all. He wasn't used to emotional situations. His Adam's apple was racing up and down in his thin neck as if it was after somewhere to hide, and he stood the way people do when they don't know what to do with themselves, one hand fidgeting the edge of the draining board. It had probably taken a lot to make him come and talk to me like this. But if you start looking back on things you begin feeling sorry for everybody. Even people like Mr G and Mr Buckley and Salvatore were pathetic in their own ways.

Let alone me.

It can make you feel terribly resigned, looking back.

'Look, all I want to say is, that letter was written half for me as well as for you. It was to say, this is how you should live, Neville, plunging in, not staying at university. This is how you should love, against the odds, courageously. And maybe he's right. But it's the kind of posture that isn't reliable. It's cerebral, not emotional. Maybe if I'd written telling him to stay with you he would have done the opposite.'

'I don't understand,' I said flatly.

He pushed a hand through his hair and you could see it was thinning.

'Did you know that Roger has a shotgun?'

'Tell me another.'

'Anna, he has a shotgun. . . .'

'I told you not to use my name.'

'We both have shotguns. Like I said, when we were 18 we made this pact. That we were going to share everything. Not just because we were friends, but because there are advantages in knowing exactly how someone else lives their life. And then that we were going to be successful. The pact was, if we hadn't realized one major ambition before we were thirty, then we were going to kill ourselves. We went through a whole rigmarole of saying we were going on a hunting trip so as to get licences for shotguns.'

'That's stupid,' I said.

'Of course it's stupid, and I stopped thinking about it ages ago. But he still talks about it being just four years away and how much he has to hurry because he's not going to accept life on any other terms. And that's what I mean by him being histrionic.'

I still didn't understand this histrionic.

'I'm going to go out to work and he can stay at home with the baby and write as much as he likes.'

'Having a baby wasn't one of the ambitions,' he said.

Then after we had glared at each other a minute, he said, 'God, it's your decision. I've told you. I can't do anything else.'

And he went.

Mrs Duckworth must have heard me crying when she came

down to put Tin-Tin out. Tin-Tin was her cat. She knocked and put her head round the door.

'Keep crying like that love and you'll make a miserable baby,' she said. 'It affects them.'

So she lured me upstairs with a promise of coffee and chocolate biscuits and we watched a documentary on pollution on the telly.

Mr Duckworth, who is paralysed from the waist down, said I really should get a telly if I was on my own. Next to a dog a telly was a man's best friend, and not half so much trouble.

Plus it would keep the kiddy occupied.

Or I could come up and watch theirs any time I felt like it, Mrs D said.

They both smoked Silk Cut and ate from a packet of McVitie's plain chocolate biccies.

*   *   *

I went through the mill of ultrasound scans and gynaccologists' examinations and being generally felt and prodded and I did a few classes of gymnastics for expectant mothers in Ealing and then stopped because it was such a haul getting there after work and I felt exhausted. I stood naked in front of the mirror in the bathroom with my hands under my belly and sometimes I felt quite proud and thrilled and other times a bit disgusted and other times again plain scared. My breasts were bigger and tight. I was going to have a baby. It moved inside me. It couldn't be true.

Dear Roger, I don't want another letter from you if you send a copy of it to Neville. I feel humiliated.

I had three dresses I wore turn and turn about and my backside filled out as well as my belly and men stopped turning round to look at me in the street – which wasn't actually the relief I'd imagined it would be. Because I wondered now whether I would ever ever get my shape back again. According to my book, the baby was about the size of a traditional style telephone receiver, and I imagined giving birth to a telephone receiver and picking it up and hearing Salvatore spell his name the long way.

I rubbed cream into myself. A cream for my belly, a cream for my tits. Would I love my baby? Would he love me? Would he be a she? And what would she look like? Would she be beautiful? Would she be ugly? And I thought it was terrible how you can't even imagine your own baby, how it has to be such a terrific act of trust, every single baby that's born, all those nine months not really believing it, not able to imagine what on earth will come out. Because it seemed impossible that it should all go well. Every last little organ, every fingernail, every eyelash. How could it? It would take a miracle. And I remember thinking once, if it all came out right, then I'd go to church with Mum every Sunday without fail for ever (I'd stopped going of course since my belly started showing, even though the vicar had said to Mum how he'd be the last to throw the first stone).

I had a dream where I gave birth, only when they showed me the baby it was Mrs Duckworth's cat that had been killed the morning before under a removals van. I woke up and lay there in the black dark, the kind you can feel pressing on your open eyes, and I tried to imagine a real birth and how perfectly natural it was and how it would all go exactly the way they said in the book. But the dream had left such a strong image of this nurse showing me a black cat wet with blood that I couldn't. The nurse was Mrs Duckworth carrying Tin-Tin across the street after it went under the removals van and saying if only it could suck my milk it might still be all right.

When there are two of you, you laugh about dreams like this.

My mother brought the baby clothes at last and an old pram that needed the rust scouring off in a few places and she said I absolutely must move back in with them and it was making my dad quite ill with guilt that I'd felt I had to walk out on them like that. He kept asking what they had done to deserve it.

Stick together was the thing, she said. Nobody was ashamed of me.

She had put on less weight than me though. I wasn't eating chocolates or anything, was I?

I could have Brian's room if I wanted, she said. She was sure he wouldn't have minded, Brian had always been generous and what was the point spending half my salary on this dump?

But I told her no.

Next morning the postman pushed something through our letter box and I rushed to the door. But it was only a letter from the public library to say that *Natural Childbirth* was five months overdue and what was I going to do about it?

I had the baby and it was agony. It felt like I screamed for hours. As soon as the contractions really got going I forgot all the deep breathing exercises and things and just screamed and screamed; it was like trying to shit a pineapple; so that in the end they put me under sedation and I can't say I blame them really.

They brought me the thing in the morning, a boy, and I didn't know what to do with him at all. I felt so embarrassed in that big room with all the other mothers all older than me, examining their nipples and wanting to know how many stitches everybody had had, and their husbands dropping in every couple of hours to fuss around them and ask if there was anything worth eating back home in the deep-freeze. My baby was tomato red from howling, with sticking-out ears, and he didn't seem to have the slightest interest in sucking me.

Mum came straight after work and said it had Brian's nose and she hadn't screamed once at either delivery.

*   *   *

I went home. I went alone in a mini-cab with the baby wrapped in a woollen shawl Mrs D had hunted out. Bobby.

I put him on the table and changed him the way they'd shown me at the hospital and made myself a cup of tea. I sat tight and cradled the mug in my hands.

I had a baby. He was on the table. Gurgling.

Roger had sent flowers, Interflora. 'Love, ME', the tag said. I hunted out a jar at the back of the cupboard.

I breastfed and listened to LBC. On the hour, every hour (LBC, not the feeding, though it felt that way sometimes). Two weeks, three. Day and night. I pushed the pram in the park and it was November with a scent of first frost and burning leaves. When Jackie came round I hid all Roger's letters.

Dear Anna,

Of course I'd never have sent copies of those letters to Nev if I'd known you'd ever hear about it. I'm pretty furious he told you. It's just that we made this pact years ago and I've always stuck to it. Everything. I've sent him absolutely everything. It was an experiment really. To see what happened if you told somebody else absolutely everything, so that they could psychoanalyse you and let you have an informed opinion on the way you were developing. I'm not putting this very well. We were young when we started doing this and I suppose there are some naive aspects to it. But I still believe the idea *is* interesting and I'd like to go on with it if you don't mind. The point is, it makes for a constantly heightened consciousness. And for conflict too. Conflict is life in a way. I mean, it's self-defining. It pushes you one way or another, channels your energy, forces you to develop. There's a bit in Nietzsche where he says, 'Don't talk to me about not arguing about taste. All life is an argument about taste.' And that's what Neville and I do. We argue about taste. I think in a way I only left university because of what I discovered through this relationship with Nev. It has crystallized my ideas. I know it must be hard for you to understand, but I'll try to explain it all better when I get back.

I hope the jacket was okay. Do send a photo as soon as you've got one.

Dear Roger,

Jackie came round last night and brought a rattle for Bobby, only he wouldn't touch it. He's too young still for toys. She flounced about all over the place, you know how she does, saying I should go to the rent control people and then to the social security office, because there must be some special deals for unmarried mothers (it's funny hearing yourself categorized like that). She was wearing one of those tight skirts which only show how big her thighs are, plus about a ton of make-up. But you could tell she was jealous about the baby, because he's such a darling with his pixy face and blue eyes. She said she wouldn't mind having one herself, but she couldn't because Mr G would go into tilt if two of his secretaries went and took maternity leave. What an excuse! Still, she changed his nappy for me, for practice she said, and we both had a laugh over his dinky little wee-wee.

You remember I told you they fired Beatrice? Well, now it seems they've got somebody new. Wendy. A bit of a prig according to Jackie, only in the typing pool on false pretences while she gets herself promoted to one of the other departments. Salvatore and Mr B are both fighting over her already it seems. Anyway, I asked

Jackie if you were back and she said no and you were getting on so famously at the office there that she thought you might stay permanently. Oh Roger, when are you coming back? I dream about you so much. You can't stay away much longer. I'd come over and visit now if only I had the money. But I don't, and it would be terribly difficult with Bobby. I ache for you, Roger, I really do. I feel my body ache. Please give me a date when you're coming back.

By the way, Jackie says everybody at the office thinks I'm being terribly secretive and everything not saying who the father is and maybe I'm covering up for somebody important or rich who's paying money into my bank account. 'Prince Edward,' I told her, 'only if he doesn't pay a bit more into my bank account I'm going to tell everybody.' We both had quite a good giggle really. You know what I am when I get together with Jackie. They're going to be so amazed when you tell them!

Then today my dad came, of all people. I couldn't believe it because it's the first time he's visited me in the bedsit here or showed any interest at all. I thought he was just going to be his normal morose, gruff self, complaining about me not going back to live at home, but after a bit he started picking up the baby and things and rocking him back and forth, counting his fingers and calling him 'Bobbsy do-dah' and tweaking his little nose. I could hardly believe it was Dad at all. Anyway, before he left he went out to the car to get me a present and it turned out it was one of those glass lamps with that funny treacly liquid inside with the big bubbles in it which just keep rising and falling and hypnotize you. It's quite a nice marmalade orange, which is good because the room needs some colour and I can see I'm going to waste hours staring at the bubbles going up and down.

Now Roger, about copying those letters and stuff and sending them to Neville. What I can't understand is this.

When you write a letter like that, like that wonderful one you wrote to me when you told me you loved me and everything and how you couldn't separate a person from their smile, it seems as if the words must be perfectly natural, as if they must come straight from the heart without thinking. So how could you calmly and coldly remember to feed a carbon into the machine before writing them? That's what seems monstrous to me. I just don't understand how a letter can be sincere and passionate if you're making carbons. It's like being in the office. So please, please don't send him any more of the letters you write to me. Even if it does mean breaking this 'pact'. He told me he'd be happier if it was broken. Anyway, it's *me* you had the baby with, remember?

P.S. The jacket's wonderful, but he'll have to be about 2 before he can wear it!

I thought one thing I wouldn't do when he came back was ask him whether he'd had an affair with anyone else. As long as he came back.

My mother said she'd give the lad real aggro and hellfire if ever she saw him.

And then the funny thing was that when finally he said he was coming, I felt quite thrown. I'd got so independent I suppose. And if my letters didn't sound as outraged as they might have, it was maybe because I wasn't really having too bad a time of it in the end. I was managing, for all the getting up at night and the complications shopping. I felt quite proud with the baby really and you could see people had a kind of grudging British respect for you, looking after it on your own.

Unless it was just cold feet. Thinking the whole thing would be decided one way or another now. Win or lose.

*   *   *

TUESDAY MARCH 2ND 2 o'clock.
Alas! Natalie cried at the airport. Sighs, tears, sobs.
Dearie me. Terrible. Much worse than with Anna.
Biblical hairtearing stuff. Wow! Women's emotions. I
feel a real bastard, naturally, and rather badly miscast for
the part. I mean, if it didn't bother me that would be
one thing. It would be okay. But instead it tears my
heart up and I start promising things, silly things, and
that makes it all worse and worse instead of getting
things over with quickly. No Byron I, obviously (all
these role models!). No, Natalie was really sobbing. The
stupid girl didn't want to let go of me. And after all
she'd said about independence! When we got near
customs I had to prise open her hands off my jacket
lapel. People were looking round to see where we were
being filmed from, probably thinking, what a cheap,
improbable production, give it a miss. Anyway, thank
God I managed not to give her my address. Otherwise it
would be the end.

So, I'm sitting here in executive class between two
typical executive-class nonentities, one the older
avuncular type, the other younger, thrusting and
paunchy, probably the kind I'm supposed to be/become.
Seeing as I'm scribbling this on company paper they
probably think I'm hellishly busy and feel a suspicion
jealous and a shade guilty because they've got nothing to
scribble themselves. Anyway, you can see they're going
to want to start talking soon. Oh God yes. They're not
the kinds who've got enough thoughts in their heads to
get them through seven hours of flying without a natter.
No, they're going to talk about airline food and films
and doing business with the Americans (if they're English) or doing business with the English (if they're Americans). BUT I AM NOT GOING TO TALK TO
THEM! I can't believe this thing I had a while back
about talking to people and hearing their voices and

picking up their rhythms and idiosyncrasies, keeping the dictaphone on in my pocket. I'm bored to death with them all. My God, people! I've heard enough turns of phrase and noticed enough physiognomical details to take me through to doomsday and anything that comes after. Anyway, the only people that really stick in your head are the ones that hurt you (or the people you hurt). Preferably the latter, though the compliment generally seems to be reciprocal. Otherwise people tend to be highly dispensable.

So, I'm going back to England. One year away. And back to Anna.

Why? Why am I settling for it? Roger Cruikshank, with all his baggage of ambitions and aiming so high? Reason it out. Put the dear heart at rest.

Well, first I absolutely must get this girl thing out of the way. Settle it. Have done. I'm 26. I do have ambitions. I want to prove I can do something and I need time to concentrate, for Christ's sake, without sentimental fuss Women waste time. On the other hand, I can't live without sex. I find myself just seized by these atrocious desires. It's really too bad. Take the American affair. On a purely intellectual basis I knew perfectly well to steer clear of Natalie. She was nice, not unattractive, admirable and fabulously American the way she was going about life (it could have been that that caught me a little off guard, novelty value), but obviously a mess emotionally. What a mess! I should have known . . . no, the point is, I *did* know, not to touch her with the proverbial b.p. Except that my dick is rather harder to handle than a barge pole (use that). It yearns appallingly. Top heavy. And there I was letting myself get drawn in, to flounder inevitably in the mud and tears of her messy life and wet cunt.

Strong stuff. Oh!

Conclusion: seeing as I can't do without it, the thing

is to find a good stable situation where you have it and it doesn't exhaust you. It sounds monstrous when you write it like that. But that's what it boils down to. Like St Paul, virginity is better (clean, clinical, economic – look at Neville, the virgin queer, never dared lay so much as a finger on me), but if you've got an obstreperous dick then for heaven's sake find yourself a nice wife. Anyway, all decisions are monsters, and you have to be ready to lose an arm or leg to slay them. (Could put that in the scene where Buckley lays into Mr G about his affair with Yvonne – no, too imaginative for Mr B.)

But why Anna in particular?

This is curious. Why Anna? Indeed indeed. Why don't I at least go for someone on my own wavelength, as Neville so aptly puts it (as if life together was a sort of seminar where you both have to have read the same books more or less, or it's not worth talking to each other – still, there may be an element of truth in that. Look how incredibly boring the girl's letters are – yet endearing. The mixture's explosive).

Why Anna? Aren't I committing a kind of classic, social/spiritual suicide?

Mostly because she's such a nice, steady girl.

No, this sounds terrible. This sounds like a real prick. I can't mean that. Me, who always wanted adventure.

'Roger Cruikshank, would-be Nobel, for motives of convenience, married nice, steady Miss Anna Eastwood. . . .'

I've been thinking about it for over half an hour (we're in mid Atlantic, I suppose, and they're about to show *Terms of Endearment*. Pretty terrible taste in the executive class, don't you think? *Terms of Leasing* might have gone down better), and the truth is, I do mean that, the nice steady girl bit. I mean I *respect* Anna. Respect (this is awful). I respect her in a way I don't even respect myself or Neville. Because she's honest, straight, and she loves me. (Neville's honest and straight – morally if not in his inclinations – but incapable of love. I'm capable of love, I think, maybe, but neither honest nor straight.) She even seems enormously wise sometimes, as if she were older and far more intelligent than me, rather than vice versa. As if she knew things 'of the flesh' – had a sort of secret door onto life. Like the time when I was saying how organizing your life was a question of mind over matter and she said, your mind over my matter? That was very good, it caught me right out (Natalie could rabbit on about expressionism till the cows came home, but she didn't *understand* anything). And it's not the only time Anna's done that. She's come out with two or three things that have really stung their way into my mind so I can never forget them. And of course she doesn't say them because she's smart or witty (no danger there), but because she's so totally honest she gets right to the centre of things sometimes. She feels these things. There. We've arrived. Anna *feels*. The honesty of love, you could say. It's impressive that love of hers. It's scalding. 'God bless' she wrote on that ridiculous card. She's not even afraid of writing God bless!

On the other hand you could perfectly well say that her head is full of romantic shit. It's all very well this consuming yearning at 20-oddish, but how are we going to pass the wet Sunday afternoons of our forties? This play doesn't finish with the happy ceremony.

Or shouldn't one think of such things? (Obviously, from many points of view it would be better not to think so much, if only one could avoid it. Because no amount of hedging can alter the fact that a bet is a bet is a risk. And all choosing is between risks. Something again that Neville utterly fails to appreciate.)

'I choose Anna because I love her and want her.' This

is what I should be able to say. Nietzschean. Is it true? Is it?

I love her. I *think* this is true. There are things about her. Physically first. There's no denying her supremacy there. Not that she's a sex goddess. But such an attractive simple body, and so natural with it and giving; such attractive movements, such a delightful surrendering when she makes love. What Neville doesn't understand of course, and never will, is how important it is that at least sex goes off well. It's like a head start. He just jerks off in blissful ignorance. To jerk or not to jerk must be the only decision that carries no risk at all.

(Why not make a pass at *him*, some time, blow his cover? He might even crumble.)

Unless it's simply the poignancy of our incompatibility in every other field that makes sex so intense (the one meeting point). But once you start investigating. . . . Say I love her. A test. Would I mind her going to bed with someone else?

Yes, fiercely. So, at least we have jealousy on our side. No, if I really begin to think of her, I go quite soft. Image after image. I love her. When I heard she was pregnant, I couldn't bear the thought that I should have forced such a delicate creature into something so ugly as a National Health abortion. I couldn't face the idea that I had caused such pain.

Whereas I couldn't care less if Natalie went to bed with someone else.

Or had a hundred abortions. Well . . .

Love and Want. I think I'm more sure on the loving side than the wanting. For example. If Anna didn't exist would I want her to?

This is an intriguing question. If she didn't exist, would I go out and look for her, imagine her for myself?

No.

If I knew she existed and knew that meeting her I would put myself in the situation I'm in now, would I go and meet her?

No. (Hell no!)

On the other hand, do I regret what has happened?

Not desperately. But a little.

Do I regret the baby? (YOU ARE A FATHER. ROGER CRUIKSHANK IS DAD.)

Not even that quite. Perhaps because I don't know what I'm in for yet.

But it's still better than regretting it even before I know what I'm in for.

(Who would deny it?)

(Or perhaps I'm just rather pleased with the personal life, backflap c.v. I'm building up for myself. Shelley, Byron again.)

So, love, but not want. Which should add up to the famous formula, 'loving despite oneself'. And that, insofar as it appears to add an extra authenticity to the loving side (in the sense of something surviving despite opposition), should be reassuring, if one accepts love as the critical criterion.

I don't of course.

Otherwise I would never have gone to bed with Natalie, whom I knew I loved less than Anna (if at all — are there degrees of love?). But then that is assuming that my actions are truly connected to my reasoning, my emotions and to the moral scheme which reasoning and emotions (mine) acknowledge. And it seems that nothing could be further from the truth.

Actions come out of the blue.

I have been watching *Terms of Endearment*. I can hardly imagine a more stupid plot. As if what I were living through now were somebody else's film and the director just went and had Anna die of cancer because he didn't know how to settle things between us (still, it might be the only possible solution). Then I have talked a bit to my neighbours and pretended to be the young executive (there's no saying they weren't pretending their roles too really, though I doubt it – who's to draw lines in this regard anyway?), and finally I re-read all the aforegoing rationalization and it came home to me with quite startling lucidity that my reasoning was *just skimming over an abyss*. Like this plane over the ocean (except without the direction). You can't codify these things into loving and wanting. You can't decide these things as if you were at a board meeting with every angle covered and weighed in the balance and Chairman Dick all ready with his casting vote. The truth is I'm an utter emotional mess, worse than Natalie, and the only thing that stops me sinking into the pit of despair is the supposed cleverness with which I am able to verbalize the problem.

I'm shit scared is the truth. I don't want to tell everybody at the office. I'm not going to marry her, no, I'm going to keep myself a good wide escape route. I'll give her some crap about not believing in marriage in the modern age. On the other hand, I couldn't face myself if I just went and left her in the lurch. How would I live with myself (a boyhood spent listening to Methodist sermons, maybe that's my problem), even though, seen from a certain angle, that might be the best and most courageous thing for both of us.

That's awful. (Courage!)

Anyway, you don't make decisions. You *do* things, action. Like I screwed Natalie, knowing I'd decided not to. Making decisions is delaying action. I feel paralysed.

(How boring just to be back with Hamlet again! How incredibly tedious! I must get this into the play somewhere. A terrible sense of frustration with being, after all, oneself, no less – or rather, no more. Me.)

This is why people kill themselves. Maybe I'm beginning to understand Chekhov. People kill themselves because they don't want to be who they are. And I'll do it on schedule, I really will, but not on the conditions we laid down in our stupid pact. I'll do it at 30 if I haven't managed to love or leave Anna (or whoever), if I haven't managed to get over this paralysis, this fence-sitting; if I still can't face being who I (indisputably) am.

One notes, in passing, the strong sense of disbelief that one is really alive and that, being alive, one is really in a situation with other people, a situation where one is obliged to do things, where history, of a kind, is being made and life – a new real person like myself – is generated.

Obviously anybody who uses phrases like, 'one notes in passing', at this point isn't going to do anything at all.

I hate myself.

I hate and hate and hate myself.

I've re-read this again and I just can't say it enough: I hate myself. Loathe. The truth is, when I wake up in the morning and find it's still me, I feel wild with rage.

Suddenly it's so obvious.

*   *   *

Roger came back. He landed and came straight from the airport with his two suitcases and he stayed all the night in my bedsit, in my bed, only the second night ever that we'd spent together right through.

When I think of how amazingly emotional it was and thrilling and how he cried even and seemed quite easy with the baby and bounced him up and down on his knee and called him Baby Bob and his blue-eyed scallywag and stood over me while I changed his nappy and put the dirty one in a plastic bag and carried it out to the bin, when I think of his first night back it seems incredible we didn't just go down to the registry office the next day and get married and live terribly happily ever after.

But we didn't.

In the morning he kissed me all over and said my nipples were awfully exciting the way they'd swollen up like that into great dark cherries, and I had much more bust than I'd had before, without having put hardly anything on round my hips and waist (in fact I'd been slaving away at these exercises on the carpet to get myself back to normal in time for when he came) – yes all in all I was his very lovable lass, he said, and at seven thirty he left and went back to Ealing on the bus so as to be able to get his car from his landlady's garage and drive to work in time for nine; when he could quite easily have taken the bus to work at eight thirty from near my place and gone and got his blessed car in the evening.

I cuddled myself in my dressing gown close to the gas fire and fed Bobby. It was funny the difference between expecting him and having him. When I was expecting, I had so many doubts still, about whether I was doing the right thing, shouldn't I maybe have had an abortion, should I have him adopted so he could grow up with a stable family without being illegitimate and so on – doubts that come from things people say. But when Bobby was actually there, snuffling, warm, smelly, or whatever, it was impossible to have doubts. I held him, pressed him to me, felt his skin, his weight, screamed when he sucked my nipples too hard, and he was there, a fact, a part of that destiny I had sensed and believed in (invented Roger told me later). It was impossible to think that it might have been better if he'd never been, except in the most shallow practical way, like when you think sometimes that it would be better if your room were on the first floor instead of the ground, or if your parents had been filthy rich. And it was impossible to think that I should have him adopted. Of course, logically there were millions of people better capable of looking after him than I was. Especially from the financial point of view. Even, I admit, people who could probably educate him better than I could (though not maybe than Roger). But arguments like that seemed really silly when you felt the contact with him and knew that you had made him with Roger, that he came from that love and that I loved him because of that, and not simply because I wanted children. He was part of me, to do with my life. Not that he belonged to me, but he was connected to me. We were connected to each other on a fifty-fifty basis. Even if you did feel like throwing him out of the window when he yelled half the night.

I fed Bobby, cuddling near the gas fire and listening to LBC about politics, and when he was done and I'd burped him and given him his gripe water and got him to sleep and tidied up the room and washed the breakfast things and generally done all the million and one stupid jobs you have to do before you get through to a breathing space, I thought I'd open Roger's suitcases and wash his clothes that he was probably intending to take back to his landlady to wash. It made me quite angry that he still seemed to be intending to go back to his room in Ealing after I'd told him there was no need and he was perfectly welcome to stay in my bedsit if he wanted to.

I was angry, but at the same time unusually serene. Like I said, the baby seemed too real a link between our lives for Roger to ignore it. And then it did feel such a tremendous victory for me that he had come straight to my place from the airport and that I had actually had him back in my arms after all the times I'd feared I never would see him again – and then that he had actually wept, salt tears I kissed away. It had quite shocked me.

So I opened his suitcases to wash his clothes, and almost the first thing I found was that thing he'd written on the aeroplane.

I read it through once terribly fast, kneeling on the carpet by his suitcases and shaking. It seemed so obscene, or as if it had come from another planet. Then I went to my one armchair and sat there perfectly still and read it through again line by line, trying to understand what it really said, because there were parts that I didn't quite understand. I sat perfectly still, because I thought if I moved I would fly into a livid rage and start breaking things. I gripped the paper tight and even when Bobby woke and started to yell I didn't move to comfort him but read and read that part on Natalie where he said he'd gone to bed with her despite having decided not to. I felt physically sick thinking of him with somebody else and another woman touching him naked and talking to him about expressionism, whatever that was.

Mrs D popped her head round the door and said, was I having trouble with Bobby crying so much, because she was after any excuse now to come and play with him, and I suppose when she saw me sitting there doing nothing, with Bobby in his cot yelling at the other end of the room, she must have been thinking what a third-rate, callous mother I was.

Still, she came in and said it was just post-natal depression, that was what. We should go out to the shops together to buck up.

I let her bundle me into my coat and Bobby into his pram and we walked down to Acton High Street, trying to keep our umbrellas from flying away in the wind. All the time we walked like that, with her talking about this cut of meat and that and how Mr D liked his butter yellow, I was thinking I shouldn't have let my rage be dissipated in this silly expedition. I should have got on the bus with Bobby and gone straight to the office and plonked the baby down on Roger's desk and said, here, this is yours, mate. Now leave me or do what the hell you want to do, but at least face up to life as it is.

Unless the truth was that I thought a scene like that would lose him for certain.

We met my mother crossing West Churchfield Street and you could tell that she and Mrs D were determined to become good friends, the way people on the verge of re-tiring always are, so that they won't get left too much on their own, and they fought each other over who was going to offer who coffee and a doughnut in the Greek café by the bridge. My mum won but it was closed for re-decorating.

'You are quiet today,' my mother said to me, and Mrs D explained it was just a touch of post-natal depression I was having. I wondered if she was as much an LBC addict as I was, because the night before Roger came back they'd had a panel of experts talking about just that, only in the end they'd decided it was most probably one of those names for things that don't really clinically exist, even if some people's hormones did play nasty tricks on them. But then I'd had to stay up till two or three in the morning to hear that.

'I was the same after Anna,' Mum said, 'but not after Brian,' and for about the millionth time she began to say how Bobby had Brian's exact same nose when he was born and she wondered sometimes if there wasn't something in reincarnation after all, though the vicar always said no. Mrs D said she often thought the same when she saw animals dead in the road, which was ever so sad.

I locked the door, so that when he came back in the evening he had to knock.

'You can't come in,' I said. 'Go away.'

'What?'

'Fuck off.'

'Anna!'

'I read what you wrote on the plane. I don't want you to come in.'

Half I meant it and half it was a kind of test, I suppose.

'You shouldn't have. You shouldn't have opened my suitcase.'

He was just inches away on the other side of the door.

'You can't just go around delving into other people's private property,' he said.

'I had your baby,' I said. 'I can do what I damn well like.'

'Don't shout so much, for God's sake. Everybody will hear.'

'I want them to.'

But in fact I hadn't shouted very loud at all for just that reason.

'Anyway, I'll have to come in for a moment to get my cases.'

'I put them out in the yard. You can go round the back and get them. The gate is open.'

'But Anna!'

A short wait, then he said, 'Christ, it's raining, they'll be ruined!' and he dashed out of the front door to go round the back.

I stood by the back door which was glass with a ruffled lace curtain over. He came into the yard and picked up his two wet cases, stood a moment hesitating. Then came over to the door.

'I know you're there, Anna.'

His voice had to be low, of course.

'Just let me in for a minute and maybe we can sort this out.'

'Like how? By pretending you never slept with her?'

'Just let's talk about it, for Christ's sake. Let's be civilized.'

'Who's the one who doesn't know how to be civilized, writing horrible things like that?'

'Oh for God's sake, Anna!'

And so I opened.

If I think back on it, it wasn't the business with this

Natalie that had really shocked me in what he had written. I mean, in a way I had been ready for that. I'd guessed it and I could even understand it – a sort of fling almost, a holiday-style fling, before coming back to me. I could forgive it. I'd already decided to forgive it. It was sick, but I could take it. It was even reassuring in a sense, or I could twist it into something reassuring. Yes, he'd had his fling, men will, so long as they're not Malcolms – but in the end he had come back to me.

No, it wasn't Natalie, but the tone of everything he'd said that had eaten into me. How could he talk about things like that? I mean, in that way? How could he talk about solving his girl problems so that he could get down to concentrating on the things that mattered? How could he say one moment that he loved me and then another go on about his dick being harder to handle than a barge pole and if I hadn't existed he wouldn't have wanted me to? I loved him dearly, I really did. I loved his hair and his eyes and his face and the way he was made. I loved the way he pushed his hand into his hair. And I wanted to go on loving him, because it would be so hard to stop. The moment he was back, standing there in front of me, my independence had vanished. I loved him and loved him. It was just that after reading those sheets of paper I felt spat on, dirtied. And that was what mattered. Not Natalie in particular. After all, she was on the other side of the Atlantic now.

But it was Natalie we talked about, as if by deliberate conspiracy. Suddenly it seemed there was nothing easier to talk about than Natalie.

He came in, smelling of cigarettes from work, and stood meekly by the door not even trying to embrace me, knowing that I didn't want it, and he said of course I was perfectly, perfectly right, and what could he say? He had acted like a typical male bastard and there was no way he could excuse himself. He had acted like Mr G would have acted.

'Tell me about her,' I said.

He shook his head. It was finished, he didn't want to think about it any more.

'No, tell me,' I insisted. 'Is she tall?'

'Taller than you.'

'And pretty?'

'She's okay. Look, Anna, what can I say? If you knew the way I feel about it, but . . .'

'Maybe you should go back to her.'

He shook his head and pushed his hand into his hair. When he was going to say something, I interrupted.

'You mean she's more clinging even than me?'

And I said, 'You know I feel spat on, Roger, spat on.'

He went through the little kitchenette into my room proper and stood by the cot. He looked at Bobby and as I followed through he said he didn't know what to say to me. He had no excuses. I had read in his letter how much he hated himself. God, how he hated himself. If I had any sense I'd just show him the door. He wished he'd never gone to America. He wished he'd never met me if all he was going to do was cause me pain.

He was really at his most earnest, the way he said this. You could see he really did wish it. His face was hurt and as if he was asking for help. We stood there watching each other.

'Stay here, Roger,' I said. 'If we live together we'll start to think and feel together. There won't be this endless tugging apart. I still love you.'

He swallowed and his eyes were watering. I couldn't cut my losses was the thing. I couldn't do it. I had invested so much in Roger. To say, Go away, would have brought the world down.

'I know there's not much room, but I phoned Mr G today and he said he'd be happy to have me back next month. Mrs D says she'll look after the baby for a few quid a week now he's weaned. If you want you can leave PP and write here all day while I'm at work. I mean, you can do what you really want to do. My salary will easily pay the rent and shopping. Even petrol at a stretch. What else do we need?'

He stood quite still over the cot.

'We would be so *happy*, Roger.'

'I know,' Roger said. He had cried one tear down his cheek, but now he came out with a small wry smile that just wrinkled up the corners of his mouth. I remember it perfectly even now, a smile that might have been sardonic and might have been penitent – or maybe he was only trying to stop himself crying more. Then he said, 'I'll leave my suitcases here then.'

'Promise,' I said. 'You'd better be serious.'

'Promise.'

When he said that I dashed across the room and hugged and hugged him and I wanted him to lift me a bit and make me fly round and round him like we'd done once before, only there wasn't space in my bedsit. I was suddenly quite mad with relief and with thinking it was going to be all right despite everything, as if somehow he hadn't really written what I'd found in his suitcase, as if a part of me refused to believe it. It was only a nightmare. So we loaded Bobby in the rusty pram and went down to Acton Park and he whirled me round and round on the grass. He really did seem honestly really happy, with tears in his eyes, saying how delightful I was and how generous to forgive him and how my love was contagious – a contagious disease, he said – and before going back home we dropped into the pub whose name I always forget by the level crossing and had a celebratory drink.

We were getting ready for bed when he said the only problem was he had already paid his rent right up to the end of May.

'Who cares?'

He would talk about it with his landlady tomorrow.

'She's got the hots for you,' I told him. 'When I saw her

that time, she said if she was a bit younger she'd make a pass at you.'

In the middle of the night then I woke and found him lying stiff and rigid on his back. He couldn't sleep. Every time he started to doze he had this terrifying nightmare. Not anything visual, just an appalling sense of paralysis inside his head, so that he had to fight himself awake again, and sometimes it seemed he would never manage to wake. He would die.

Now he was scared of closing his eyes even.

I touched him and he was sweating and goosepimpled together.

I got up and checked Bobby and came back to bed and stroked his hair. 'Roger the Dodger,' I whispered in his ear. 'Dear Roger, sleepy Roger. Sleepy, sad, bad Roger.'

We were naked and I stroked him and some time around four o'clock he got to sleep.

I thought I would never be able to rely on him, to trust him; he was so slippery; but at the same time I felt older than him somehow and as if he needed me to look after him; and I thought I was going to keep him, definitely; I was going to keep him, because I couldn't face my life otherwise. If I couldn't keep him, then I would tear the whole world apart. I truly would do something mad.

*　　*　　*

If there's any part that's difficult to make sense of it's what comes next. And I'm not going to be able to do it. I can see that now. I wonder sometimes even whether words have that power. When I think of all the words that passed between us, of all the words I listened to in those days on the radio, or the words I read in books and magazines, they all seem so hopelessly, uselessly light, as if they were ready to float up in the air and disperse like a kind of gas. While the things that were happening inside us, to us, between us, the things that changed and destroyed us, these things were unthinkably heavy, crushing and suffocating, and they didn't seem to have anything at all to do with things as light as words.

I said to Roger once, what was the point of talking if we never got anywhere, and he said words were a consolation. You could tell the agony, he said, roughly by the number of words people felt bound to spend on something.

That must be why babies cried so much then, I said, because they had no words for consolation.

He laughed and tickled me and said what witty turns of mind I had sometimes. He was always looking for any excuse to laugh and tickle me and forget it all. But then so was I for that matter. Neither of us really wanted to think about what was going on, for fear of having to do something about it.

For a week after he came back from America he slept with me every night and he brought a few clothes and things from Ealing in his two suitcases and pushed everything under the bed, except for his workclothes which he put on a coathanger in my wardrobe.

He had sorted something out with the landlady, he said, about money.

And not to worry about what he'd written on the plane. Honestly. It was just him playing Hamlet. Just a pose. He was perfectly happy, really. He'd have to be an idiot to leave a girl like me. It had all been a terrible mistake with Natalie.

When he found me depressed he tried so hard to cheer me up it was painful. He said things like, 'Of course I love you.'

What about his papers and things? I said. I thought maybe we could build a kind of desk by the window with some plastic milkcrates and a piece of wood.

When he had a spare moment.

But at the weekend, instead of completing the move in, he went to see Neville in Cambridge.

I would have liked to have gone to Cambridge myself, because I needed a break from Acton and it would have been nice to sit out on the green of his college if the sun was warm enough and let Bobby roll around in a grass that wasn't full of dog dirt like Acton Park. But Roger said he'd never be able to book us both a room in college with a baby during term time. I could have pressed and said okay a hotel then, a man with a diesel Passat could afford a hotel for the night, couldn't he? Only he so obviously wanted to go alone.

About ten minutes after he'd gone Saturday morning, with me just preparing for a trip to the laundrette, my mum barged in without knocking and demanded to know where 'that man' was.

Mrs D had told her it turned out. That there was someone with me in the house.

'Out.'

She was breathing hard, her nostrils flaring, but funnily enough, although she had obviously come to give him a pretty hefty piece of her mind, she'd put on her best skirt and jacket to do it and brushed back her hair and lacquered it stiff and put on piles of eyeshadow to make her eyes seem larger than they were, because my mother has small eyes in a big face.

'Then I'm not moving till he gets back.'

She sat down hard in the armchair and folded her arms and started a sort of determined silence.

'He's not the one.'

She looked at me.

'The father is the one who came that night when I wasn't in, the short, darkish one. This one is different. He's blond.'

I don't suppose it had ever dawned on my mother that I

might have had more than one lover. I think in her whole life she only ever had sex with my dad and she had naturally cast me in the role of the victim, as everybody else had if it came to that, and even if they were right, I didn't want to be thought of as one. I suppose I had decided, if he wasn't going to tell anyone, it would be better if people thought I was modern and independent.

'I'm sorry, Mum,' I said, 'but there's no point in shouting at this one.'

'You're a little scrubber then,' she said.

I had my arms folded too, standing by the screen wall that partitioned off the kitchenette. I said, 'Brian had a million girlfriends and went to bed with all of them and you never batted an eyelid.'

'How dare you!' She stood up. 'How dare you talk about your brother like that!'

Her face was boiling red and stretched tight round her lips and for a moment I thought she might be going to slap my face. But then she just dissolved into tears and was sitting sobbing on the edge of the bed. 'You're glad he's dead,' she said. 'I know you are, you're glad he's dead and you always were. You never cared a button about Brian. I don't understand you. I don't understand how you can be so cruel. And just when we were all so happy and your dad was going to retire and . . .'

She broke down completely in great wrenching sobs, so that I had to sit down beside her and comfort her and find her a box of Kleenex. After a while the baby joined in too and so we ended up with him on our knees rocking and cuddling him and tweaking him on the pixy nose and bouncing our legs up and down while my mother sniffled and half-laughed and cried all together and began to worry about having ruined her make-up with all those tears.

'If he comes in now, what ever will he think of me!'

'Who?'

'This bloke of yours!'

'He's not coming back till Monday.'

Then she wanted to know what he was like, and seeing as I'd told her he wasn't the father, I started telling her all about Roger and described him and how intelligent he was and ambitious and handsome. Telling her about him, I fell in love with him all over again and I felt happy and desperate together, because I was winning in a way, he was living with me now, only it was all wrong and sick too with those awful things he'd written, like I could never be quite sure.

'Nice of him not to mind.'

'What?' I said.

'The bloody baby!' She could kill that other bloke, she said, she couldn't understand why I had defended him so long, why I had had the baby.

I shrugged my shoulders.

Still, it was Brian's nose he'd got, she said, to a 'T', that was something to be thankful for, and after elevenses she pushed the pram down to the laundrette with me.

*   *   *

I didn't see Roger till Monday morning when I went back to work for the first day and of course in the office we couldn't talk because there was that old pretence we had started that had to be kept up because he still hadn't told anybody. Often I thought it was crazy of me not to tell anybody, but the problem was I was trapped in the thing now. If I told people, they would want to know why we hadn't told them before, and then they would pull Roger's leg so much and make life so hard for him that he would leave, the office, me and everything. They would want to know why he had been such a bastard as to stay in America while I was having the baby.

It was only when I thought of other people looking at our relationship that I began to feel just what an incredible bastard Roger by anyone else's standards had been. And if I thought of that I saw I couldn't tell anybody because they would immediately think me mad for staying with such a bastard, they wouldn't understand the way I couldn't see life without him. Anyway, I didn't want other people knowing and criticizing us. Because the truth was it was all so fragile what there was between Roger and me that if we brought it into the light I was afraid it would dissolve and disappear, like those mummies they say they can't open ever, or the Stone Age paintings in caves that nobody can go and see, because if you did they would fall apart. Our love was there, I knew it was, but unrealizable somehow; we couldn't seem to make it part of everyday life.

In the beginning we hadn't told anybody about us because Roger wasn't proud of me and because he thought in a way if you didn't tell people about things then they hadn't really happened, or at least, you could get out of them at a moment's notice without too much bother (he even used to say it would be easier for me if we split up if nobody knew) – but now it was different, now we couldn't tell anybody anything because something *had* happened, the baby, and people would want to know why we hadn't told them before. Which didn't bother me that much, but he would never survive it. He would disappear.

They had put in a new filing system in the office and I spent ages wandering around trying to find where to file things, crouching down to look at the bottom shelf and then standing up suddenly and having to grab hold of a desk to stop myself keeling over and fainting.

I thought it was a crime, not telling anybody, a sort of secret sin that got worse and worse and more and more dangerous the more we kept it secret.

Everybody was kind and asked how the baby was and Jonathan told me with a perfectly straight face I was as deliciously sexy as ever and how he found it difficult to concentrate on his work now I was back. He said it with

Mr Buckley right there in the room and even he managed a faint smile along with a snort and asked me whether I was having any problems while he dialled a number on the telephone.

The only way, I thought, would be to have Roger say he had fallen in love with me after the baby. But that was terrible.

And what would I tell Bobby?

Or we could move away a million miles!

Except if we both left PP it was somehow difficult to imagine us being together at all.

'Here we are again then,' Jackie said in the pub at lunchtime. 'And never the twain shall meet.' She nodded toward the execs.

Wendy asked me for about the tenth time whether it was a boy or a girl. You could tell she didn't like being relegated to having lunch with the secs. She kept looking around in a hungry, eager, intense sort of way with her eyes wide and straining a little, sure sign of contact lenses. She had thin artsy fingers with bluish nail varnish and she twined and twined them together on the table.

'Wendy's got a crush on Crukers,' Jackie said.

'No, I haven't!'

Crukers was their nickname for Roger.

'You always time your visits to Design for when he's there.'

'I bloody well don't.'

'You do.'

'Well what if I do? He's the only decent male around here.'

'Going to start coming to the disco again?' Jackie asked me.

But I told her no.

'We're sick.'

'I know.'

'I mean not telling anybody.'

'I know perfectly well what you mean.'

'When you phoned from America you said . . .'

'I know what I said.'

'Because if we . . .'

'You don't have to spell it out, for Christ's sake, you think I haven't been through it enough times myself?'

'But why, Roger, when . . .'

'Don't go on.'

'I love you, Roger, I . . .'

'I know you love me, I know all about your love.'

He wanted to go out for a hamburger, but I didn't, because Bobby was sleeping. And because Bobby was sleeping we had to talk in low voices. When we wanted to scream.

'Have a good time with Nev?'

'No.'

'Why not?'

He shrugged his shoulders.

'Let's go out.'

'But Bobby . . .'

'We'll take him then for fuck's sake. It won't be the end of the world.'

'If you set up your desk here, you could work while I read. I thought that's what you wanted to do in the evenings.'

'I can't work in the same room with somebody else.'

'I'm not somebody else.'

And I said, 'It's silent as the grave here, Roger. You'll never find anywhere quieter. I was terrified on my own here, honestly. That's why I went and had the security lock put on.'

I was terrified of anything that wasn't rose-tinted, he said.

'That lamp is awful,' he said, 'with those bubbles. Truly awful.'

We went to Strand-on-the-Green in his Passat and sat at one of the pubs, watching the river.

'Do you feel embarrassed having people think you're the father?'

'I am the father.'

He had carried Bobby all the way from Kew Bridge in his arms because prams were the end according to him. He wouldn't be seen dead pushing a pram.

'I know. But does it bother you?'

'Not specially. So long as I'm not pushing a pram.'

We began to drink quite a lot and he seemed to relax. It was fascinating the position we were in, he said, and that was what Neville had completely failed to appreciate. 'He never wants to push life anywhere.'

'Oh, I quite like Neville. Except when he started insisting you were just an actor and hysterical and so on.'

'He said I was hysterical?'

'Something like that, I can't remember the word exactly.'

'Anyway, everybody's an actor; it's just a question of settling into your part.'

'I'm not acting,' I said, and he said, very softly, on the contrary I was the best and most convincing and sexy actress he had ever met and that was why he had gone and fallen for me, and he leaned across the table and gave me one of his little kisses on the corner of my lips, which we called Cruikshank specials.

'Musk might be cheap, but it's pretty damn sexy,' he whispered in my ear.

'Have you fallen for me, Roger?'

'That would seem to be the word.'

I watched him.

'Then why not move in for good and leave PP and we'll get started on this new life?'

Passing, an elderly man bent down to say goochy-goo to Bobby where he was sitting on my lap.

'Little cracker you got there, love,' he said and Roger said, 'I will.'

This was the thing, that he could be so romantic, so much what I hoped, and we seemed to boil over together from these horrible armed tensions into frantic lovemaking; so that, that night, after kissing and squeezing and petting with Bobby held awkwardly between us under Gunnersbury railway bridge, he drove back like a maniac for us to dive into bed together, and he had this idea that I breastfeed Bobby while he stayed in me from behind, only I wouldn't let him. I said every time he drove it was like we were in a getaway car.

Speaking of which, he said, there was some loot he'd forgotten in the boot. A pushchair and some other things for Bobby and a dress for me. 'Got them in Cambridge.'

'Oh Roger!' I said.

I was so ready to see things look up.

*   *   *

He brought some paper and wrote on it in the evenings on the kitchen table, but he didn't bring his typewriter and he didn't want to set up the writing table I had suggested.

What he did do though was buy a lot more things for Bobby, toys and so on, to stimulate him, he said, and he read articles in magazines about educational toys. Anyway, I couldn't be expected to face the whole burden economically.

I said if any of the furniture or things I had put up bothered him, then he should rearrange them as he chose; I mean, if he didn't like the orange lamp with the bubbles and so on, then I was quite happy to hide it away in a cupboard and just bring it out if Dad visited, which would be once in the bluest of moons.

But he said he didn't want to impose. If I liked it, which I obviously did, then I should keep it there – and I did like it, so I kept it. And I kept on reading *Princess Daisy* too, because I had to read something when he was writing, seeing as I couldn't listen to LBC, and when he poked fun and I said, okay, suggest something else, as long as it's not T. S. Eliot or Kenneth Galbraith, he said why not try a book he had called *The Collector*, by John Fowles; so I tried, but it was a horrible, disturbing book and I simply couldn't read it, physically couldn't, like I can't bear the news stories when they talk about children who are raped and killed.

He said I couldn't face reality and I said the point was I didn't want to if I didn't have to – there must be nicer books to read that were good – and anyway, wasn't it him who was always telling me that everything there was was imagined?

The reality I had to face was what others imagined, he said.

'What are you imagining, Roger?' I asked. 'Tell me and I'll face it.'

But he ignored that. Anyway, he said, there was a great deal of difference between aiming for, or imagining, relationships that really worked and wasting my time with pie-in-the-sky-Princess-Daisy-loving-husband-at-the-end-of-the-permissive-experience crap that stank frankly.

I said, 'The only thing I want is to be happy with you, Roger.'

And later, in bed, I said, 'Maybe Neville's right though, maybe we're just not compatible, I mean, all these arguments we have and never telling anyone.'

'Neville's never seen us in bed!' he laughed.

'But we can't spend all day in bed.'

'We can think about it.'

'When I'm reading,' I said, 'whatever it is, the thing that matters is that I'm in the same room as you, being quiet together, feeling us breathing together with Bobby sleeping there.'

He said if he put the things I said in a play, people would groan they were so soppy.

'Then they must have pretty dull lives if they never feel like I do, because sometimes I just want you and want you so much it's like I'm going to burst.'

We made love.

Again, there was this about Roger and me: we made love every day, even when things were terrible between us. In fact, the worse they were, the longer and more complicated and hungry and exhausting and hopelessly exciting our lovemaking became.

Once he said it was like two people adrift on a boat who could only eat fish, but they were going to make damn sure they ate every kind of fish and cooked it in every way possible and picked the bones clean as a nun's small mind.

He liked those kind of odd comparisons and he got up in the middle of the night to write that down. He had to search in his suitcases for his pen and notebook because he put them away there every evening where I wasn't supposed to read whatever it was he'd written.

I hated his suitcases. One day I would burn them.

*   *   *

At work Salvatore said I was looking awfully tired and was I ill? Jonathan proposed to me at the end of a letter in answer to someone's complaint about our services.

'I'm perfectly serious,' he said when we were standing in the alcove where the photocopier was.

'You've got a girlfriend already.'

I couldn't help giggling with Jonathan. He must have shaved round that little moustache every day, it was so neat.

'I know, I've seen you with her.'

'That's right, but now I'm thinking in terms of a wife, sweetheart. And with you we'd already be through the weaning stage. Family man without the hassle.'

'I might take you up,' I said.

'When they fire me we could go to Australia.'

'Jonathan! Don't be so stupid!'

'If you knew how much passion there is in my stupidity. I really go for young mothers.'

And he leaned over the copier and kissed my lips, quite firmly. 'You're a darling,' he said and went.

It was a pass, I suppose, and not unpleasant. The funny thing was how light and easy life seemed to sit on everybody's shoulders but Roger's and mine.

Over our typewriters, Jackie said, 'Making any progress with Crukers yet?' and Wendy told her to mind her own business.

Wendy sucked a whole packet of Callard & Bowsers Butterscotch every day and Roger said it must be destroying her teeth.

But then she said the thing was he probably wasn't available. He had a girlfriend already.

'No!'

'I've asked him to loads of places and he doesn't seem specially averse. I mean, he smiles and everything and says he'd like to, but he's just not free.'

'Never heard Crukers mention a girlfriend,' Jackie said raising her eyebrows at me.

I said, nor had I.

'I thought he was one of those proverbial handsome and holy bachelors.'

Wendy said, on the contrary, Roger was just the kind to have a little girl tucked away somewhere he didn't want to talk about, someone who did her duty and served her purpose and left the great man free to get on with his ambitions. Because according to her he obviously wanted to be a director one day.

She laughed after a moment and said, 'I'll sort him out though, just you wait.'

'I told you you were after him.'

'Not much else for a typist to do.'

Wendy came every day dressed to kill these days with silver gloss tights and little velvet jackets and there was a sort of competition between her and Yvonne for the best-dressed flirt in the office, only Yvonne won hands down, I thought, because she took it seriously, while for Wendy it was a bit of an ironic joke and you felt she might change into jeans and a sweater any time. Anyway, Yvonne had the kind of breasts they show in magazines and Wendy didn't.

Salvatore and Mr Buckley had a terrific row with Mr G about Yvonne because he had got her a company car the same as theirs and she didn't have to do any travelling for the company at all.

'Except when she goes to Boots for Mr G's you-know-whats,' Jackie said.

Salvatore wanted Yvonne fired right away so he could have Wendy in his office and Mr Buckley didn't because he was hoping to fire Jonathan first and get her in his. Only Jonathan is one of those people who somehow never quite get fired whatever they do, because he is good at his job in a relaxed, unambitious kind of way and he doesn't get up anybody's nose but Mr Buckley's.

The more I thought about Jonathan in fact, the more I liked him and I had a wistful feeling sometimes when I thought how nice it might have been if I'd fallen in love with him instead of Roger. Stupid, meaningless thoughts. Like on rainy days when you think how nice it might be if you lived in the Canary Islands or something. I tried to think how he would be naked if ever I went to bed with him and how I would tell him all about my affair with Roger and he would laugh and say how stupid we'd been taking everything so seriously and how he'd never really liked Roger, though the truth was they were always playing squash together in the lunch break.

I felt quite stable and normal in the office, and in a way I suppose I liked work for that. Even when I saw Roger I felt perfectly controlled and calm and I wrote letters and hunted files and gossiped behind Mr G's back and Salvatore's and Mr Buckley's, quite as if I was anaesthetized. When I was at the office it seemed that the tension building up at home simply dissolved, and in the fluorescent light there and the tobacco smoke, the phone always ringing and typewriters chattering, the smelly carpets and heaps of things to file, it was hard to believe that sense of crushing pressure there always was between Roger and me in the evenings, the feeling you might explode any moment and do something mad.

We rented a television so that he could watch *Play for Today* and a couple of other things it was important for him to watch. We rented it in my name, but he paid the rent and the licence because he said he couldn't have me spending money on things I wouldn't have spent it on if it wasn't for him.

And while he was about it he might as well give me something for food and rent, he said.

I refused. I said I loved him and I wasn't going to accept money for cooking him fried eggs a few times and having him in my bed.

The only arrangement I would accept with money, I said, would be if we opened a joint account and had done.

He sat with his forehead wrinkled and his workshirt open, twirling a pen in his hand, and I was watching the half-smile creeping up his face, when the doorbell rang. Then he was like an animal in alarm. The smile froze, the free hand pushed into his hair and held there and his eyebrows raised sharply into an urgent question. I shrugged my shoulders. By the time I'd got back from the front door with my mum, he was gone. Out the back.

I waited up till the small hours, but he didn't come back that evening. I watched telly since he'd rented it, right up to closedown and then listened to LBC, in the dark. About sex for the over-sixties. I remember wondering if I'd ever get there. I felt so exhausted inside and beaten.

At work first thing he slipped upstairs with the pretence of getting something typed urgently and he left a note on my desk that said, 'Sorry, forgive me, Rog.'

*　　*　　*

'If you left the office it would make it all so much easier. Anyway, I hate having to listen to the others saying how they're going to pick you up and everything.'

He was watching football. He had begun to watch all sorts of programmes as well as the ones he 'had to watch'.

'I'm not leaving the office.'

'But Roger . . .'

'That new thing I was writing has just been turned down.'

'So? Everybody gets turned down.'

'Exactly,' he said, and he said he wasn't leaving the office until he had some sign of success. He wasn't going to make a fool of himself.

'You mean get trapped with me?'

'No.'

'But if you don't take a risk. . . .'

'I know,' he said. 'If you knew how I know.' Then he said, 'I'm losing my impetus writing-wise. I can feel it.'

'So what happens?'

'Indeed!'

'So let *me* at least leave the office and you pay the rent. So we can end the pretence.'

He swung round and stared at me, and the intense blue of his eyes was hard. He scratched his front teeth slowly. 'You? You'd just mope at home and worry that I was getting off with Wendy or whoever.'

'Not if you promised you weren't.'

On the television somebody scored.

'Crap.'

'I'd have another baby,' I said brightly, trying to be cheery. 'I could get into it. Anyway, you can't just have one.'

'So then everything would have turned out exactly as you wanted.'

'Why not? I'd be happier if you were successful though. Oh Roger, don't give up, and don't feel trapped by me. Enjoy my love,' and I went and folded my arms round his neck and kissed him.

Stoke were the most boring team in the world, he said. He could never understand why they showed Stoke on television. Even if they won the World Cup all by themselves, he would never watch Stoke.

'You are watching them.'

'They're my home team,' he said.

The following evening he wasn't at work when I left and he didn't come to the bedsit that evening. It became a regular thing. Some evenings he just didn't come. He went to the room in Ealing he was still paying for and wrote. That's what he said. He had only brought the two suitcases of clothes to my bedsit so he must have had plenty left back there. And even the suitcases he hadn't unpacked. He never told me which evenings he would be coming and which he wouldn't and at first he used to apologize, but later he said it was my fault if I sat at home doing nothing and moping. Even if they were in love, people should be independent. It was a crime to want to be dependent. I was too passive. None of this would ever have happened to us if I wasn't so passive. I should amuse myself, for Christ's sake. I should learn how to drive so I could go out in the evenings.

'With whose car?'

He would help me buy a Mini if I learnt how to drive.

I began to cry, thinking of the other Mini. Which was stupid, but there you are.

'And the baby?' I said.

He suddenly flew into a temper and started shouting.

'You never let be. Never! Christ! You never let be forcing me into the shape you want me to be.'

'Leave me then, damn you,' I said. 'And take all your rotten filthy stuff with you. Fuck off. I hate you.'

And I said, 'I felt perfectly independent when you were in America, thank you very much. I didn't have any trouble amusing myself at all. You should never have come back.'

'She's telling me,' he said.

He got up and walked out, slamming the door, but he didn't take his suitcases. I saw him pause at the door a second, deliberately deciding not to.

As soon as he was gone, I regretted it, what I'd said, and I sat in front of the television rocking Bobby and eating my lower lip. Bobby was a disaster in the evenings. He whined and was irritated and there was nothing you could do to settle him unless you gave him that Calpol stuff that has aspirin in it, but Roger had said under no circumstances was I to give him aspirin unless he was actually ill, otherwise I'd turn him into a moron.

'If you were around a bit more,' I said, 'you could take him off my back and I wouldn't feel like giving it him.'

The funny thing was that instead of going mad, like on this other occasion, he'd agreed with me that time. He said I was right. 'You know what's wrong with me,' he said. 'I'm a shit, that's what.'

'I didn't say a word,' I said.

'I'm not fit to be alive,' he said. He was serious, but smiling at the same time. 'With a personality like mine. They should suppress people like me, before we can do too much damage.'

'Nobody minds a bit of damage,' I said, and I dragged him off to bed; only as soon as we'd got going, Bobby started yowling. I wanted to leave him to cry, but Roger never would, not even for five minutes. He didn't want his personal petty pleasures to be responsible for anybody else's traumas, he said.

Except that seeing as only Mummy could quiet the brat down, it was me had to get up of course.

I thought over all this in front of the TV the evening he walked out. I thought about the two sides to his character, the one that exploded at me and the one that exploded at himself; and I thought about my own character, the way the more he was a bastard the more I somehow wanted to mother him, even though I felt like screaming too - I tried to think all this over clearly and make some sense out of it, but I couldn't fathom it at all. Only you could see we might both end up in a home if it went on much longer like this.

He didn't come to work. He had phoned in sick. For Thursday and Friday and the whole of next week. He didn't come to see me in the evenings either and he didn't take away his stuff.

At lunchtime once, I phoned Neville from the office to ask about him.

'I thought you'd split up,' he said.

Neville was kind and sympathetic, but distant, as if he was a doctor talking to a patient he knew was dying.

'I can't live without him,' I said. If it hadn't been the office where anybody could come in at any moment I would have cried and cried.

'What's the use of him saying he's sorry if then he just goes and does it all over again?'

Roger was a strange person, Neville said, and if he seemed deceitful sometimes it was only because he didn't know what he wanted.

I said I was fed up of hearing shit like that, and he said, 'I can imagine.'

When I next saw him, he said, to tell him that his thesis

had been accepted for publication, and I think I said, congratulations.

*   *   *

On the second Saturday I asked Mrs Duckworth if she would look after Bobby an extra day for an extra few quid and I took the bus to Ealing.

It was a warm summery day and I put on my hat that he'd given me and a shortish red skirt and yellow blouse with a necklace of fake pearls and a spray of musk. Before going I spent nearly an hour with the curling tongs and changed three pairs of earrings. I was furious. With myself. With him.

At the bus-stop I remember wondering if there was anything at all left of me outside this obsession. I hadn't seen him for nearly two weeks, yet every waking moment I'd been thinking of him – thinking of screaming at him, loving him, cursing him, comforting him, listening to him – so that it seemed maybe I had no personality apart from him at all.

'Oh, it's you,' his landlady said. 'He's out.'

She had people in. There was a hearty man's laugh came from the sitting room. Husband number three, perhaps, if she had found someone healthy enough.

'Can I wait?'

She looked over her shoulder.

'I could go up to his room,' I said.

'Yes, I suppose that's all right. He's probably only out for the paper or something.'

When I started climbing the stairs, she said rather tartly, 'I see you know your way then.'

The walls of his room were bare as ever, only it was untidier than before. He had got out all his clothes from the cupboards and put them in piles on the armchair and then rumpled them all up. Probably when he was planning to come and stay with me. There were two boxes on the floor, half-full of books, but there were still some books on the shelves too. Had he ever intended to come lock, stock and barrel?

I stood by his desk and read the sheet of paper in his typewriter.

G: Got that, success lies in singlemindedness.

Harry: For somebody with two minds, singlemindedness is suicide.

G: (laughing) Haven't you read that bit in the Bible. If thy right eye offends thee, pluck it out, damn it!

Harry: I'm trying to forget what I read in the Bible. My parents used to bore me to death with the thing.

G: You're making a mistake, Harry – there's a lot a salesman can learn from JC & Co. The first thing being, offer people what they want. If they're scared of dying, offer them eternal life. And if our clients want impossible deadlines, offer them them. Even if you can never meet them in a million years. But get the work.

Harry: Okay, I lie. And when we can't deliver?

G: For heaven's sake, lad, once you've fucked a woman you've fucked her, right?

That was where it finished. I couldn't quite see the point of it. It all seemed rather boring and improbable to me.

I found my face in the mirror. The blush of the make-up seemed dangerously fake, the eyebrows looked bushy. My lips were thin and tight, not sexy at all.

I remembered what he had said when I cried once: 'This is just any girl's little tragedy.' And I said, 'What help is that?'

It was him who usually looked in this mirror. He looked at his straight nose and white teeth that he scratched with his fingernails; he saw the blond hair he tousled by accident

134

even when he wanted to look smart, his strong neck with the muscles that slid over each other and the smooth, smooth skin of his cheeks going into the finest prickling of beard round the mouth.

Why couldn't it turn out well for me? I was ready to give everything.

Then the fear that I might never lie next to him ever again, never slide my hands over him, rub my face against him, that fear gripped me like something quite tangible, made me weak at the knees, nauseous. Like a change of temperature in the room, a drop of a hundred degrees. I was shivering and sick. I wanted him by me, kissing me his Cruikshank special kisses and all the little things he did and I did when we made love. It was irrational and over-whelming and I had no resistance.

Standing in front of the mirror, I started to take my clothes off. I slipped the necklace over my head and undid my blouse and when my breasts came free out of my bra I felt terrifically excited and anguished together. I went close to the mirror to look at myself and I thought of him sucking me and squeezed myself.

I slipped off all my clothes and got into his bed which wasn't made and lay there staring at his empty walls in the summer light through lace curtains. I turned and pressed my head into the pillows and my skin was screaming.

Downstairs somebody guffawed and the landlady, I sup-pose it was, gave a little shrill squeal.

What if she came up? I didn't care. I was past caring. If she came up I would tell her everything. And I began to hope she would come up, so I could tell her. As if that would help. So I could tell somebody everything.

It must have been five minutes or so before I noticed his dictaphone. It was on his bedside table with empty cups of coffee and change and bits of fluff from his pockets when he emptied them out, and there was his little alarm clock too with the beady red digital display that had always made sure I was up and out by the time the landlady came back from her cinema club.

I thought I would like my wet cunt to dribble all over his sheets, all over his room and his work clothes, so that everybody, everybody would know. So that he would stink and stink of me.

I picked up the dictaphone and switched it on and there was just a faint hum. I wound it back a way.

. . . in all the world. Click. Pause. Click. Can't sleep. This is terrible. What is it like? I can't describe it. I start to go to sleep and then this massive sensation of pressure, paralysis, angst, whatever you want to call it, seizes me, so I can physically feel my brain under pressure and I'm struggling to get out. The only thing seen is blackness and I wake up sweating and cold, my brain racing with all these problems.

So tense too. My tongue feels swollen. Always chafing against my teeth.

I'm punishing myself is the truth. The old Methodist background. I feel like one of those medieval monks flaying his back. Why?

Young man emotionally damages young girl. Common enough. Normal outcomes: young man marries girl and after period of understandable sullenness lives as happily ever after as anyone ever does; or, young man ditches girl and she, after a period of understandable deep depression, falls in love with somebody else, as is her nature.

Why can't it be the same with us?

In extreme cases the girl might kill herself.

But not the young man.

In other, more honour-conscious nations the family of the girl might kill the unobliging young man and cut off his prick and stick it in his mouth. But not in England. Not in England.

For the young man it should be plain sailing.

This is one of the hinge elements of the story after all. His casualness, her anguish. Cinch for him, Calvary for her.

Just leave! Leave leave leave! Christ! Doors are there to be walked out of.

I am torturing myself. The young man. Gratuitously. Why can't I ever seem to come out of this? This impossible mixture of tenderness and rage. I can't think of life without her body.

Or with it.

(The fact is, I need psychiatric help.)

How could she be so pure in spirit and eat into me physically so entirely? How could she be so attractive and such a pain in the arse? So truly, seriously passionate and so trashy and cloying?

I fell in love with the directness of her love for me.

If she had been a bit coarser.

If she had been a bit more devious, a bit more selfish.

But would one ever find such devotion and quality in a more complex person?

Maybe not, okay, fine – or maybe yes, who knows – but anyway, am I really responsible for my incapacity to love her back? The way she wants.

What did I expect?

Why this enormous sense of responsibility? Nobody else has it.

See how professionally Mr G chooses his mistresses. Admirable.

Get rid of the responsibility, baby or no baby. You'll only damage the thing. No responsibility. Do what the fuck you like with who you like. Sleep sound. Don't raise hopes.

Even if you're a lesser man for it.

Click. And you are. Click.

If I had a play on stage somewhere and people wrote reviews about me and invited me to speak on *Kaleido-*

scope, and so on, it would all be so much easier. If I stayed with Anna then, it wouldn't be a burial. There would be that career in front of me, that future, that prestige. And if I left her there would be so much to leave her for — and then every celebrity has a right to his little scandal, proof of his wayward, inventive character; it's just fitting yourself in the canon as it were.

But the little man is responsible for everything. The little man is crushingly responsible. He has no excuses.

And I'm beginning to get the feeling I'm a very little man. A very little man indeed.

Click.

Fight that.

Click.

It's true enough though.

Click.

Curious thing: this all reminds me of when I wanted to stop going to church and Mother and Father were so upset the only way I could see to do it was to make myself so ill they'd let me off. Except that it wasn't just a ruse. I was punishing myself for not believing, like I am now I suppose for not loving. File that for the analyst.

Click.

Oh weird, weird, weird! What a mess. Betty of all people! And just to prove I too can be tough and cynical and Byronic. Her tits! And she enjoyed it so, so much! Do it, do it, do it! A giggle of tits, I would describe it. A belly laugh, heaving and writhing.

Never felt so *squeezed!*

No wonder her poor husbands. . . .

What will I think tomorrow?

If the world didn't offer one these so convenient conveniences. If it was a more austere, responsible place. If I had told everybody from day one about Anna, pinned my colours, I would have been true, I truly would. I wanted truly to be true.

Sounds religious. Adolescent.

Now I feel like a chameleon. I never realized how many women might be ready to fuck me, how differently I might react in each case. (Wendy. A titless screw. I bet she has a really bony little pube, tight bum, a real tearing grind. Ooh! Why not? She's pushing it at you. You can almost smell it. The kind who really digs in her nails. Butterscotch blow job into the bargain. Why not?) Boundless possibilities. Boundless, literally no character, no limit, no identity. I'm not me. Do it, do it, do it!

What a magnet Anna is though, with her loving. Anna is a force for definition.

Anna.

Anna's home. Her baby.

If only she weren't so vulnerable.

If only she weren't so generous.

I would have left me ages back.

Click.

God, I'm fed up to the tip of my foreskin with if onlys.

I'm not going to tie myself in guilty knots.

I'm going to rampage.

I must rampage.

Wendy, I'm going to fuck you.

Oh yes, Wendy my well-spoken, brightly painted young thing you, I'm going to get down your. . . .

Roger came in.

I had my knuckle in my mouth, listening, and my teeth were tight on it till it hurt.

He rushed and grabbed the thing and switched it off.

He stood and stared.

I was nude in the bed.

After maybe a minute, he said, 'Well?'

I took the knuckle out of my mouth.

'I listened.'

'I gathered that.'

'To that shit.'

'Apt.'

'You've got totally the wrong idea about me, Cruik-shank.' My voice was trembling hopelessly. I felt hysterical.

He was in stylish, Saturday clothes, baggy trousers and a khaki shirt with sunglasses up on his forehead. He took them off and the hand pushed into his hair. His teeth chewed at a lip.

'I'm not a glass angel. I'm a little scrubber and I want to get laid. So get going.'

He said, 'Leave off, Anna. This isn't *Last Tango in Paris*.'

And he said, 'Haven't you played masochist enough?'

I just started to sob. 'Oh Roger, Roger, Roger.' Great awful sobs. 'Why? Why? When I love you so much, Roger.'

He sat on the edge of the bed and after a moment put his arm round me and pulled my head to him. 'Anna,' he started. But I grabbed him tight. 'No, don't say anything, please, Roger, don't say anything.'

We held each other a while and I half-calmed down, wiping my face on his sheet. He pulled away and put his head in his hands.

'Really, you should leave me. You heard the tape.'

'I know, but I'm not going to.'

'I'd murder me if I were you.'

'Well you're not,' I said, 'Lucky, isn't it?'

Then I said, 'Make love to me, Roger.'

'But. . . .'

'You said you couldn't live without my body.' I watched him. 'That's what you said. Anyway, you owe me this, even if it's the last time we do it, you owe it me for being such a shit.'

He turned and looked at me sitting up nude there with my tits sticking out; and I could just see from his face he wouldn't resist. I could see it and it gave me a sudden odd strength. I knew him so well, my Roger.

In bed afterwards, he said again I was a total masochist, and I said, so what? he was a total coward, and the two seemed to go rather well together, didn't they? Anyway, there was no point in him worrying any more about hurting me. Because he'd already done it and the world hadn't ended, had it? He gave up, he said. It didn't matter what he did, I always came back. And I said, 'Of course, it's the only way I've got of punishing you, Roger.'

Perhaps the world *had* ended, though, he said, what about that? and we stayed in bed making silly listless pointless conversation all afternoon until we made love again and went back to Acton.

Looking back, I wonder now if maybe we didn't enjoy how sick all this was. Perhaps it was amusing watching the hole getting deeper and deeper.

Even if, skin to skin in the sheets, I knew I had done the right thing.

★   ★   ★

Bobby was crawling and I bought a blue rug to cover the part that was just floorboards. Roger insisted on christening it with a fuck and he didn't put down a towel at all and didn't want me to clean up the stain.

Times had changed. He gave me money and I took it. He came some evenings but not others and he wasn't agonizing any more and I wasn't fighting. We went out together sometimes for walks with Bobby and there was the famous, wistfully happy Saturday morning when he dragged me into the car showroom with the baby on his arm and sat at the wheel of the XJ making brum-brum sounds. It was his nearest to being a father.

If we met anybody these times we'd agreed to say we'd met by accident.

'You haven't got a shred of self-respect,' he said, and I said, 'Snap.'

But we never met anybody.

I thought, if we'd lived in a little town, none of this could ever have happened.

Bobby was very big for his age and full-fleshed and bouncy. I don't know how come, but it made me feel very proud. I suspect Mrs D was feeding him all day. He gaga-ed and banged his fists and snuffled infant snuffles.

'He'll call you Daddy one day,' I told Roger when we came out of the showroom.

'Certainly time is on your side.'

'You weren't really going to kill yourself at 30, were you?'

'There seems no point. I feel like I'm already dead.'

Yet he was full of fun that Saturday.

I hated him for all this, of course, but at the same time the funny thing was that I thought we were settling down at last. I mean, there was this terrible anger hidden away inside me somewhere, something really dark and awful, but it didn't seem to stop me going on loving him. Perhaps loving and hating somebody weren't incompatible after all. Anyway, I'd decided I would go on loving him right to the end, whether I hated him or not. I would go on loving him till he gave way. I was determined. Because I was never going to do him the favour of leaving him, like he wanted. No, if he wanted to leave me, he could find the courage to do it himself. And I thought he was bound to give in before I did, because I was certainly the stronger. Otherwise he'd have been gone long ago.

Life was pretty confused, I suppose, with thinking things like this, and then drinking champagne in bed sometimes, the nights he was there, and pretending we were the world's greatest lovers. Mad things made him feel he was halfway alive, he said, and he said there were all kinds of ways for couples to be together. We didn't have to follow traditional patterns. At least we'd kept things intense.

At the office Mr G called me down for a private conversation. He was doing a survey to see what people in the office thought of him. Was that reasonable? He thought so. If I objected, I could always refuse to answer his questions. On the other hand, if I answered with perfect frankness, he would never hold anything I said, however unpleasant, against me.

I said yes. I was feeling ill to tell the truth. Like I needed more air, or had a blockage in my throat or something.

Because he respected the opinions of ordinary simple girls like myself and Jackie, whereas he was fed up to the back teeth with the pontifications of Buckley and the cloak-and-dagger work of that Machiavellian Salvatore.

'Would you like a coffee?' he asked. 'A good one I mean.'

'Nadia,' he spoke into a white box. He never waited for an answer when he made offers. 'Two coffees from across the road and a couple of Danish pastries too.'

He rubbed his hands and grinned in his beard the way he would and lifted one gangly leg up on a chair.

'What I want to know is, do you – people in the office, that is – do you mind me having an affair with Yvonne and do you mind that I do it more or less openly? I mean, do you all feel offended?'

'*I* don't,' I said. 'It doesn't seem any of my business.'

'Quite. But are people in the office angry?'

'We make jokes about it,' I said.

He frowned. 'You don't think it significantly reduces efficiency?'

'Maybe a little bit. Not much. Anyway, you need something to gossip about in an office.'

'It doesn't reduce staff respect for the management?'

'Everybody knows who you are, Mr G. I mean, you're you.'

'Right.'

'Perhaps one or two people are jealous. Especially the men.'

And I suddenly realized that Roger had always been jealous of Mr G's happy-go-lucky mistressing. Always. Which was why he had to make those scathing comments. And in another way jealous of Neville too. Of each man's serenity.

'But on a moral plane? What do you think, really?'

I thought. He was looking down at me with his fingers fiddling in his beard.

'Does your wife know?'

'Generically.'

I took a breath. 'I suppose I think you're a bit of a pig,' I said.

'Right, of course.' He seemed to be getting excited.

I said quickly, 'But then at least you don't try to hide anything. You're not furtive.'

'What Buckley wants?' he laughed. 'Horrors no. It's just the inevitable battle of the sexes.'

'I don't think it's inevitable. I don't see why you can't stay with. . . .'

'Oh it is,' he cut in. 'You'll learn that. I just can't understand why Buckley and Salvatore keep on at me so much about it.'

Nadia came in with the coffee and pastries.

'So, that's that. Tell me about yourself. All well? How are you getting on with the baby?'

'I'm fine.' I was feeling so dizzy I had to hold on to the edge of the chair.

I ate my pastry and went upstairs clutching the bannister. A half-hour later I threw up on my way to the bathrooms and Jonathan took me home in his Toyota.

'The offer's still open,' he said. 'Any time you need someone to claim paternity.'

144

And he said, 'At least you could come out for a dance with me one night.'

'Do you really like me, Jonathan?'

He turned and smiled. 'I really like you, Anna.'

I didn't invite him in though, because I didn't want him to see Roger's things around.

*   *   *

I had thought Roger would be fearfully angry, but it was worse. He was cynical, offhand.

'It must have been when I came to your room. I didn't have my stuff.'

'Well, at least we know you're good at one thing.'

He was looking for socks in his suitcase, dressing for work.

'It takes two.'

'Sometimes I wonder.'

And he wouldn't say anything else.

After breakfast I said, 'So what shall I do?'

He was playing with the breadknife, twirling it round in his fingers, and without looking up he shrugged his shoulders.

'Suit yourself. I'd have an abortion if I were you. One is already a life sentence.'

I felt my eyes full of tears. 'I can't. I can't do that, Roger. It would be like giving up. Like admitting there's no future between us.'

'I thought we'd already given up.'

'Then what are we *doing* here?'

I felt myself trembling and my voice small and strangled in my throat.

'The sixty-four-thousand dollar question.'

'If I had an abortion now, I should have had one before. How can we go on making love after an abortion? I can't bear it. Roger, please! Please change. Love me.'

He waited. He must have waited five whole minutes without a reply or a caress. We sat over the breakfast table and in the silence we heard Mrs D upstairs wheeling Mr D into the lavatory.

'Your love has destroyed me,' he said quietly. 'I was never like this before. If you hadn't loved me, I'd be fine. I'd have left you without any problem, like I've left other girls.'

Bobby began to cry, his thin long wail of hunger.

'You're sick you are,' he said. 'You're sick the way you draw everything into yourself. Love is sick the way it never never lets be. You're sick because you can't adjust your trash literature expectations to the world as it is. To me as I am. And you eat your little heart out with that sickness and suck blood out of everybody else.'

And I said, 'But I love you, Roger. You know I do. I love every inch of you. It's just that I'm tired of not knowing how things will be tomorrow. How I will manage.'

The baby was wailing and wailing. It was like talking in a gale.

He said I would never know how things would be with him. He couldn't be pinned to any walls. He wasn't the person I loved, he was somebody else. I loved somebody I had mistaken him for. Yes, it was all a question of mistaken identity. Like when they hung the wrong man. And he began to hum that Bob Dylan song we had a recording of by Bryan Ferry: 'It ain't me, babe. No, no, no, it ain't me, babe.' He was laughing. 'It ain't me-e-e, that you're looking for, babe.'

'Leave then,' I said, but he said, what was the point, what was the point of leaving if I always came running back to him?

And he was right.

'We're obsessed,' he said. 'Tough luck. You know you can't live without me. Somewhere along the line we must have deserved each other.'

He sat with one hand clutched in his hair, twirling the knife with the other, whistling again – 'It ain't me, babe' – and behind him was the new blue rug I'd bought to stop Bobby hurting his knees on the floorboards and the rented TV with the lamp on top and orange bubbles that my dad had brought the only time he came to my bedsit.

'I'm pregnant again,' I screamed. 'Christ, I'm pregnant, and that's all you can say.'

He went on whistling.

I was weeping and furious and quite at the end, and I stood up and stumbled round the table and grabbed the knife from his hands so that it was pointing at him, at his chest.

'I'll kill you then,' I said, not meaning it at all.

And he laughed and said, 'Oh, I shouldn't do it with the knife, lovey.'

He looked into my eyes and his own were smiling and smiling. Our arguments didn't touch him any more. He didn't care. He wasn't even tense. 'You're not strong enough for the knife. I'd use the shotgun if I were you. It's over in Ealing. I'll get it for you. Do me a favour. Honestly. Been meaning to kill myself for years.'

He looked into my eyes, and looked away to gather the crumbs from his breakfast plate, as if I wasn't worth a moment's attention. He was grinning. In the whole wide world I was his only triumph. He didn't feel responsible any more. He could ignore me.

So I killed him. Not knowing I was doing it. Not meaning to. If I'd meant to, I'd never have had the courage. My anger just rose and exploded. I lost control. I pushed the knife hard into his clean shirt that his landlady had laundered because he still took his laundry to her and I killed him and then I took Bobby out the back to calm him down and after he stopped crying I made my sandwich and took Bobby upstairs and went to work, snapping on the security lock with its two great barrels that spring into two deep holes.

I closed my eyes and ears and heart to Roger. I didn't see or hear him at all. I really don't remember anything. He had fallen face down, that's all – I stepped over him – and he wasn't moving and the blood was going black in the blue of the rug. That's all I remember.

★   ★   ★

At six-thirty Salvatore popped his head round the door and said enough was enough, and I covered my typewriter and laid everything out neatly on my desk.

Doing his rounds, Mr Buckley said, 'Make sure to have a good weekend. Up to anything special?' and I said, not that I knew of.

I phoned Mrs D to say I'd be back late and clocked out.

Jackie said she would have invited me to her place, only she had an important appointment with someone.

Which meant Ian.

She always went to Ian's when Dereck had a darts match, but she didn't let on it was Ian by name because it wasn't exactly anything to boast about. If it had been Roger, she would have said Roger.

But Roger had never said Anna. He never said he had an important appointment with Anna.

I'd killed him. Just like that.

'Lend me a tenner till Monday, Jackie,' I said. 'I lost my purse.'

At eight o'clock I was on Waterloo Bridge. I wasn't quite sure how I'd got there. Somehow I hadn't gone to speak to anybody. Just got on the tube at random. I should have gone to the police, but I didn't. I suppose because I'd realized I could never explain, and because they wouldn't want to hear anyway.

I was guilty.

And if he was too, that didn't help matters. They would take Bobby away from me. Bound to.

I stood on Waterloo Bridge and leaned on a wet balustrade, watching the city at twilight. I had stood here once with Roger.

Roger used to say that London was the only city in England. He said the throb of its life drew you towards it. Until you realized that you could never get inside that life you had imagined. It was a myth you had made. The city attracted you like light attracts a fly and then there you were with a million other flies buzzing blindly against a window that never opened. And the throb was only the buzzing of those blind frustrated flies.

I used to love it when Roger talked. My head was full of things he had said. In a way maybe I had fallen in love with his voice and his earnest talk. He said so many things. But he never *did*, and he never said things that were *actions*, as he put it when he talked about his plays. He never said, 'This is my girlfriend, Anna. This is my baby.'

He slept with that landlady, Betty, any number of times, just to remind me how independent he was. He said, 'Listen to my dictaphone when you feel like it. Keep up to date by all means.'

Maybe he slept with Wendy. Maybe he even slept with Neville to screw him up like he said in that stuff he wrote.

There was a low London sky and drizzle and lights pricking on all over the city, which was always there and humming and throbbing, but which you were never quite part of, as Roger and me had never quite been part of each other: when I realized I had my hat on. His hat.

I took it off and threw it out into the river. It sailed and tumbled and the wind blew it back against the bridge a couple of times and then it fell beneath.

I could follow it. I could jump if I wanted. But I wouldn't. I already knew I wouldn't. In the end I was too

149

commonsensical for that. And I wouldn't go to the police either. Perhaps I had been wrong about love and destiny. Perhaps it was all a girlish stubbornness, a refusal to accept defeat. Perhaps I should have compromised way back, aborted, fallen in love with someone else. Dear Roger. He was dead on my rug.

I walked to Waterloo Station and hunted in the telephone directories.

(With a kitchen knife of all things! It was incredible. That I could have had the strength. Me. And all the blood.)

'Hello. Jonathan? It's me. Anna.'

'Oh, Anna. Hello.'

'I want to go to Australia with you.'

There was a pause.

'All of a sudden?'

'At least to a dance then.'

'That sounds a trifle more manageable. Where shall we meet?'

'There's just one condition.'

'Ah, guaranteed chastity?'

'No, nothing like that. You have to help me get rid of a corpse.'

'You what?'

As always, nobody expects to be surprised by me.

'I'll explain when we meet. You will help though?'

He was face down. I wouldn't have to see him.

'I've always said, Anna, you've got a terrific bum.'

'Oh, be sweet, Jonathan,' I said in a flirty, little-girl voice I'd forgotten I had.

'I think you're a darling.'

'Do you love me though?'

Again surprise, a pause. 'I wouldn't go that far, sweetheart, but I might.'

'Meet me at Acton Central then in forty minutes.'

I thought, if he listened to my story in a pub or something and we could get the corpse into the Passat and move it without Mrs D seeing, then nobody would know. Why should they? Roger had done everything to make sure nobody knew he lived with me.

He always said it would be easier for me that way in the end.